Border Patrol

Rod Galindo

v1.2

Tin Can

an imprint of Wordwraith Books, LLC

This is a work of fiction. Names, characters, places, and incidents are products of the author's imagination. Any resemblance to actual events, places, government organizations or persons living or dead is purely coincidental or used fictitiously.

ISBN-10: 1-946921-03-3
ISBN-13: 978-1-946921-03-1

Wordwraith Books, LLC
705-B SE Melody Lane #147
Lee's Summit, MO 64063
www.wordwraiths.com
@Wordwraiths

Cover art by Rod Galindo

Rod Galindo's website *www.rodgalindo.com*
Rod Galindo's Twitter *@RodAGalindo*

Dedication

*This story is dedicated to all the faithful scientists, engineers, communications experts, and everyone else who continue to keep the dream of our wayward robotic ambassadors alive.**

I'd also like to dedicate this story to my fellow Kansas and Missouri Army National Guard soldiers who deployed with me to the Hashemite Kingdom of Jordan. You always kept my compass true, and never faltered in your Army Buddy—ahem, Warrior Companion—duties. Can I get a HOOAH Santa Fe? ☺

* Note to all Voyager subject matter experts, engineers, physicists, honest-to-God rocket scientists, and astronomy teachers/professors:

I respectfully request that none of you drive over me with a Martian rover when you find I completely blew it on certain technical aspects of this book. Specifically my numerous speed and distance calculations, my understanding of simulated gravity physics and advanced propulsion concepts, and last but not least, the technical specifications of the Voyager spacecraft and the (hopefully feasible) technical specs of my fictional *Explorer Two*.

I had intended to plead for an invaluable "beta read" from über-educated men and women like yourselves to help make this book as technically accurate as humanly possible prior to publication. Because let's face it, Internet research can only go so far, especially when it's done by a career soldier who likes to think of himself as an amateur "armchair physicist" thanks to being inspired at a young age by 1970s science fiction. Alas, *another* military deployment significantly pushed back this story's development and completion, and an unstoppable book launch window—namely the 40th Anniversary of Voyager 2's launch—subverted my best intentions. That said, please feel free to e-mail and chastise me regarding any gross errors you come across in the story, and I will diligently strive to correct them in a future edition (perhaps a re-release on the 50th Anniversary of the launch date?)!

Thank you,
Rod Galindo, Armchair (id est holographic) Physicist and Astronomer
rod@rodwerks.net

Thank you for checking out my short story, I hope you enjoy it!

Allow me to send you the first three chapters from my upcoming novel, **Distress Call.**

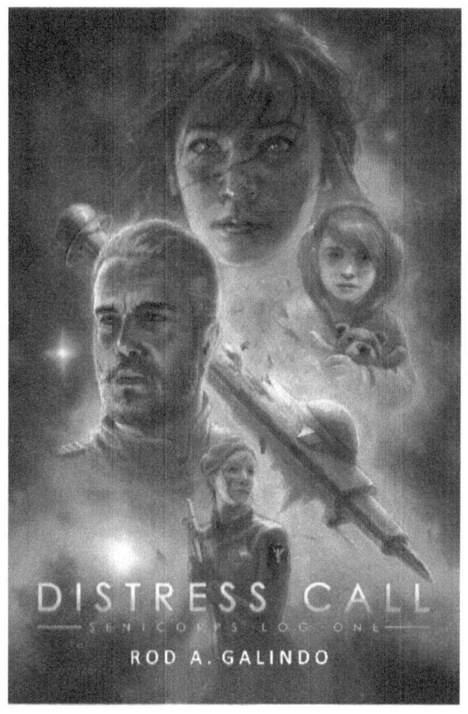

Simply hop over to RodWerks.net/SecretSC and tell me where to send it! ☺

For more information on upcoming projects and books, please visit RodGalindo.com

ONE

Sparks shot in all directions. Circuitry popped and crackled. Alarms blared.

"Scales, shut your station down!" Commander Bouchard ordered.

Jack "Scales" Scalia threw two switches and mashed his fist on a bright red button, and the navigation station went dark.

The sparks died down, but the popping continued. Donnie "Darko" Bouchard slammed into the rear bulkhead of the command cabin in the zero-G environment. He ripped a bottle of compressed CO_2 from its wall mount and maneuvered to brace himself, lest he go zooming backwards as soon as he activated the extinguisher. The fire safety system had done all it could, and prevented a fatal fire in the command cabin, but the crew wasn't out of the woods yet.

Don pulled the safety pin and placed his feet on the wall behind him, standing directly on the colorful logo that read "Space X", "Virgin Galactic", and "NASA" in big, bold letters, plus sported the flags of all the countries involved in their deep-space mission. He aimed the mini bottle rocket at the navigation station, and pulled the trigger. The extinguisher nearly jumped out of his hand, but in seconds, the station turned white, and the crackling dropped to a minimum. As Don watched and waited for more popping, the white coating evaporated before his eyes. He heard two more small pops, then nothing but the blaring of alarms and annoying beeping that signaled a whole lot of hard work ahead of the seven-strong crew. "Anyone hurt?" he yelled.

Murmurs of "no" and "fine here" reached his ears from both his navigator and science officer.

Science specialist Ray Isley executed a graceful backflip and darted through the rear hatch, "I'll be down at my station!"

"Roger, X-Ray." Bouchard kicked off and floated back to his station in the small cockpit, to the right of the pilot's chair. He didn't bother to sit down among the plethora of screens surrounding the chair. His gaze locked onto the one that kept him up to date on the status of the small nuclear powerplant towards their spacecraft's stern. All the "bars and bubbles" were still green, as usual. *Whew. So far, so good,* he thought, and moved on to the health status of six delicate devices housed in the belly of the spacecraft, intended for defensive purposes. The bubbles on them showed green as well, and the word "DISARMED" next to each one allowed Don to exhale and relax a little. But only a little.

Another screen informed him that alarms were blaring in every habitable area of his ship, which amounted to about one-half the length of their six hundred-meter-long vessel. As if he wasn't fully aware already. "Shut off that racket!" he hollered to no one in particular.

Scales spun upside down, twisted his body 180 degrees, and flipped a switch on the panel opposite the now charred navigation station. Silence flooded the cabin.

"Pearls, M&M, Treads, Mag-Lev, you guys all alright?" Bouchard asked, speaking into his wrist watch, which was a mini command station of its own.

There was a moment's pause before a perky voice with a slight Mandarin ring erupted across the small space. "Mags and I are okay, Commander, we're in Storage Unit Twenty-One!" Medical Specialist Melodi Meng-Scalia replied. "We're a little shaken up, but no one's hurt. Mags is on his way to check on the engines. We got a lot of red lights down here!"

"Roger, M&M, glad to hear it." Don said. "About you, not the warning lights!" He glanced over at Scales, whose cheeks puffed up as the man let out a long, slow breath, visibly relieved upon hearing his wife was okay. "Mags, I know you're on your way; I need to know how things look down there as soon as possible."

"Rrrroger!" Mission Specialist Lawrence "Mag-Lev" Liev replied in his slow drawl. His deep-woods, southern-Missouri accent was about as far from his roots as a Russian could get. "I'm on my way to Ion Control, runnin' a Propulsion Systems Check on my watch as we speak. I should have the results by the time I get there. Just passed the 'gas station'; no leaks in the xenon tanks, or at least none that the sensors are registering. I'll have to do a one-by-one inspection when I have a minute, just to be sure. Moving through Nukie right now, he looks green, thank God." A pause. "Huh..."

"What?"

"Oh, it's probably no biggie. It's just that he's running at 27.3 megawatts. Haven't seen the generator pushing that much juice, well, ever. Not even when we began the trip! Hold on... Okay. It looks like the smart system is giving us more power after detecting the system failures, knowing we'll need it to repair the ship."

Don zipped through a menu on one of his screens. "Yep, I'm reading the same thing up here, Larry. How long can it run that hot?"

"Honestly, I don't know. It's never gone past 25. Have to do a little research and get back to you."

"Alright. And let me know when your system check completes."

"Willll do!"

"Has Pearls checked in yet?" Bouchard asked Jack.

Scalia shook his head.

As if on cue, a dark form zipped into the cabin at a high rate of speed, narrowly avoiding a collision with the navigator. "Sorry!"

"Speak of the devil," said Bouchard, smiling.

"Hey, careful!" Jack hollered. He couldn't have dived out of the way in zero-G even if he wanted to. "Those bionic legs of yours will shoot you right through the cockpit one of these days!"

"Don't be jealous," said Adrienne Perle-Liev as she slammed hard into the back of her cushioned pilot's seat, but latched onto it before it sent her flying back towards Jack. She then executed a somersault, and landed square at her station.

"I'll give you a seven point five on that one," said Bouchard. "You about lost your grip on the chair that time. But I blame Jack for distracting you."

"Thanks. What did I miss?" she asked in her noticeable Bangalore, India accent.

"Oh nothing," Don replied. "Just me acting all heroic and saving the ship again."

"So, same old, same old?"

"More or less."

She smiled big, throwing switches left and right to bypass whatever she could in an attempt to shut off the red and amber warning lights on her console. The glow from the screens around her made her pearly white teeth glow in stark contrast to her dark skin. The effect was short lived; her smile faded as she studied the screens in front of her. "Just as I feared. We've lost acceleration."

"Yeah," Don replied. "I hope that's all we've lost." There was one final person to check on. As Commander, he had to check on his crew first, his family last.

Pearls looked over her shoulder. "So did you guys see them, too?"

Don held up a finger to Adrienne, indicating she hold that thought for just a moment. He didn't know who the "they" were to which she was referring, but he was certain whatever she had to say could wait until he acquired some peace of mind in regards to the status of their starward home, not to mention the safety of his wife. "Treads, where are you?"

"I'm here in the ring, Donnie," Brea Treadwell-Bouchard replied. "Bloody hell, what are you doin' up there?" Her charming British accent was music to Don's ears.

"Just trying to keep us afloat at the moment," he replied. "Are you okay? How are things there?"

"I'm peachy. But a few things down here aren't. Most of the mess is just books and non-breakables, but one of X-Ray's experiments is a lost cause. And I'm sorry to report one fatality."

Bouchard's heart stopped. "But everyone reported—"

"We lost Scales II."

Upon hearing the name, Don started breathing again. "You scared me for a minute, babe."

"Oh. Sorry, pet."

Bouchard turned to the pilot. "Sorry, Adrienne, I know how fond you are of all the little critters we brought along. But look at it this way. Scales II made it a hundred and twenty-two AU! He traveled farther than any other fish that ever lived on Earth! Except for the other five we still have, of course."

The young but clever former fighter pilot pressed her lips together and took a deep breath. "Poor little thing." Adrienne had been given the call sign "Pearls" by her peers either due to her name or her beautiful white teeth—Don wasn't sure which, but he guessed probably both. "Well," she said, "maybe I can talk them into a little goldfish ménage-a-troi to keep the population up?" Then she quickly added, "Larry, if you heard that, don't be getting any wild ideas."

"Wouldn't think of it, darlin'," came Lawrence Liev's voice over the speaker system.

Bouchard shook his head. "Understood on the goldfish, Brea. Anything else damaged?"

"Just my pride. Thankfully no one saw me take a tumble down the ladder."

"Well now that you just told us about it, we'll have to screen the video at dinner."

"Go ahead," she challenged. "I'll drop a pillow and blanket out in the hall for you tonight."

Bouchard grinned at the playful retort.

"I'll be in Auxiliary."

"Roger, babe."

Mag-Lev's voice returned. "I have preliminaries, Darko. What do ya want first?"

"Top to bottom," Bouchard replied.

"Well, top would be the accelerators, I'm sure you can see from your screens up there what shape *they're* in."

Don spun his head and found the screens showing the status of various parts of the ion engines. One illustrated clearly that four of their six long accelerator tubes were damaged. The tubes in question flashed red.

"If I can't fix 'em," Larry Liev went on to say, we might as well forget about slowin' down to match speeds with Voyager, if and when we find the old gal. With less than half thrust, hell, we'd probably better think about spinnin' 'round and initiating a breaking maneuver now. Might slow down to a manageable speed by the time we're all walking with canes."

"Great," said Bouchard, lowering his head. "Pearls, Mags may be exaggerating a bit, but he's right. We'd better start recalculating our deceleration point. We'll need to spin the ship and start braking a whole lot earlier than we intended, and possibly use a lot more fuel than we originally figured as well. How far out did you last say Voyager was, Scales?"

"In Astronomical Units? If it's still speeding outward at 3.3 AU per year, she should be at five hundred twenty-eight by now, and add another ten by the time we reach her," Jack replied.

"So we have to bring this baby down to 55,000 KPH using only two ion drives, and we've only got about four hundred AU to do it in."

"Even if we still had our constant rate of acceleration," Pearls said, "we wouldn't have begun decelerating for another year and a half. Now that we're at a constant speed, and at only..." she checked a readout, "a measly 210,000 KPH, we probably won't have to adjust our numbers by much, even with only two engines."

Don made a motion to the screens in front of her. "Give the old man a warm and fuzzy, will you? If Mag-Lev can't get the other four drives fixed in the next twelve months, we'll need the new numbers anyway."

"No problem, Commander."

"Go ahead with your report, Mags."

"Roj-o! So the ionizers seem fine, the neutralizers all look good. Might have to print some more wiring. Hmm. I hope the 3D in the tunnel didn't crap the bed, I haven't had time to fix the one in the bay yet..." His voice trailed off.

That's all we need, thought Bouchard. If they were to lose the ability to fabricate spare parts, the crew really would be in pickle; there were no "filling stations" out this way—as his great grandfather used to call them—and they were slightly outside the post office's delivery area. "Got it. What else?"

"That about does it for the engines. After that, it looks like we'll need a new regulator unit on the air scrubbers. It's blacker'n my Pa's angus bull on a moonless night. Even worse than when it's full o' CO_2! Oh, and the toilet here in Ion Control is a lost cause, so I'll be usin' your and Treads' latrine from now on."

"Is the one in your cabin broken?"

"No, but Adrienne has it all fancy smelling in there. I'm a grease monkey. It's just too much. I've been using this one."

Bouchard glanced over at Pearls and chuckled.

The pilot looked over her shoulder. "Somebody's gotta keep the place proper, if I left it to him, our cabin would smell like a fraternity and a garage had a child."

Don chuckled to himself.

"Have you had time to look into how long a fourth-generation Siemens GX2161 nuclear generator can run at ten percent over capacity?"

"I have. It should be fine for several days. But it might be best if we give 'im a little breather after that. Just to be safe and all."

"What does that mean?"

"Oh, we take him down to three-quarters power for a little while. Dim the lights in here a little, ease up on the luxuries if we have to."

"How long is a little while?"

"A week should do it."

Don considered it. "Long as we can keep the magnetic field and the life support at full power."

"Of course."

Bouchard nodded, even though Liev couldn't see him. "Alright, Mags, gather what you need for pulling apart the damaged accelerators. Keep me informed."

"Roger dodger."

Treads broke in. "Donnie?"

"Yeah, babe."

"I'm going to borrow a phrase from Mr. Mag-Lev himself. There 'ain't no way' Mags is using our loo."

Bouchard looked around the cabin and saw everyone crack a smile. "Sorry, Mags," he said, "but you're going to have to bite the bullet and use the fancy toilet. The Lady of the Ring has spoken."

"That's okay," replied Liev, "I'll just pee out the window."

Someone giggled on the line, Bouchard couldn't tell who.

Pearls turned to Don and spoke in a low tone, not keying her microphone implant so she could speak freely to him and Scalia. "So? Yes? No?"

"Okay," said Bouchard, "what were you talking about earlier? Did we see what?"

"The shots. Were you two in here when they hit us?"

Jack spoke up. "Shots? What do you mean? Like gunshots?"

"No," Adrienne replied, "I mean like lasers."

"Lasers?" Scalia asked. "Like from a laser gun? Did you open that bottle of champagne we've been saving for our meet up with Voyager?"

Adrienne sighed. "No."

"Then what makes you jump to the conclusion we were hit by lasers?"

"Because I was up in Observation Tower 1 when they hit us," Pearls said. "I saw the streaks; they zipped right by the dome. They looked like meteors in a moonless sky deep in the Thar Desert. Little yellow threads of light. Two of them."

"Shots!" Scalia scoffed in his Jersey accent. "Out here! Have you gone batty or somethin'? Did you stop to think that maybe they really were just meteors?"

"Meteors streak because they're in atmosphere," Adrienne spat in retort. "Last I checked, I can't breathe on the other side of this cockpit window. Can you?"

Jack didn't reply.

Don squinted through what remained of the light smoke and extinguisher dust still floating about the cabin. Through oversized windows that wrapped around eighty percent of the command cabin, he searched the heavens for anything moving amongst the static star field. "Which direction did they come from, Pearls?"

"Toward starboard. There, in Scorpio. It almost looked like they came right out of the galactic center itself!"

Don glanced to his front-right, at the dense "cloud" of the Milky Way, which stretched across the sky seemingly north and south from his spaceship's perspective. Of course, cardinal directions had little meaning out in The Black.

Scalia had floated up to the front of the cabin, and held onto the back of Don's chair. "Hold on. Do you really think she saw what she saw, Darko?"

"Why wouldn't I?" Don replied. "Pearls doesn't play practical jokes."

"Well, it's a little far-fetched, don't you think?"

"Far-fetched perhaps, but not impossible."

Jack chuckled. "You've seen too many old holofilms."

"Probably," Bouchard said, scanning all around the constellation of Scorpio, the scorpion, killer of Orion the Hunter.

"On the elevator ride down, I kept my eyes peeled for more shots, but I didn't see any. I saw part of the damage they did, but as you know the protective disc blocks a good portion of the accelerator tubes."

Don turned back to the screens around him, but before he did, he caught a glimpse of Pearls pulling up images of the ion engines from various external cameras. She whispered words of incredulity at what she saw.

Don didn't look up. "Do I even want to look?"

"No," she replied, her gaze never leaving her set of screens either.

No one spoke for several seconds while Don maneuvered through various screens describing the "health" of *Explorer Two*. Between the ship's automated systems and the efforts of the human crew, most of the warning lights had turned amber or back to green, as various damaged devices and circuitry were bypassed for the time being.

Scalia broke the silence. "So we're seriously entertaining the idea that it wasn't a natural event that just happened?"

"Those 'yellow threads of light' didn't come from nowhere, Scales," said Bouchard.

"I'm telling you," insisted Jack, "they were probably meteorites."

Perle turned in her seat and gave him a hard stare. "Meteorites? And our navigator sat right there at his station and missed them?"

Jack's voice dropped a full octave. "Micro-meteorites. Very micro."

"And what made them flare up just before they hit us?" asked Bouchard.

Scalia shrugged. "I don't know. Could be a dust cloud out there and they lit up zipping through it. Or hell, now that we've just left the magnetosphere of the sun, a hundred and twenty-two AU out, we are now fully susceptible to cosmic radiation. What Pearls saw could have been pin-point, focused blasts from an ancient supernova."

Don gave him a side-ways glance. "Only two of them? Wouldn't a whole swarm of blasts have zoomed by? Wouldn't they be zooming by right now?"

"Maybe, maybe not."

"Okay let's run this down," said Don. "Two laser-focused threads of radiation, launched from a supernova thousands if not millions of years ago, crossed precisely this point in space at exactly the same time as we did, and impacted the only equipment on this entire ship that wouldn't suffocate us, starve us, or blow us up. I'd say the chances of that occurring at random are worse than the odds of this ship turning into a potted daisy in the next five seconds."

No one so much as chuckled. Dead silence fell upon the cabin for an entire five seconds, as everyone seemingly waited to see if anything would indeed happen. Don lamented the fact his crew never seemed to understand most of his ancient science fiction references. Especially his wife. It was as if London carried completely different programs in their holo libraries than Montreal.

"Well the odds are better than aliens with laser guns being out here!" Scalia yelled.

"Really? I'd say they're about fifty-fifty right about now," Bouchard said, matter-of-factly. "Until we have more information, I'm going to assume a continued threat to this vessel, and take steps accordingly." He pointed at Scalia's half-burnt station. "Increase magnetic field to its maximum radius, and boost it to one-thousand percent of nominal."

"We won't be able to maintain that for very long, Darko," Scales notified him. "Remember last year's coronal burst? It wasn't the burst that nearly cooked all the meat in the pantry, it was our own magnetron. I'm glad Brea remembered to put the poor fish in the freezer ahead of—"

"I got it Jack," Bouchard interrupted. "Just do it. It's about the only 'defensive weapon' we have that I'm willing to use. Set it at five-second bursts, repeating every five seconds. Don't let it fall below normal power between bursts."

Jack Scalia maneuvered back to his station. "Alright. Boosting to one thousand percent."

Bouchard turned toward the pilot. "Adrienne, keep your eyes peeled. I'll bet my next paycheck something's out there. And it isn't a supernova." He eyeballed Scales. "Or meteors broken off from a bigger asteroid."

"Roger, Commander," she acknowledged.

"Boy do I ever hope I'm wrong," Bouchard muttered to himself. He heard Scalia tapping screens at the navigation station, flipping blackened switches and mashing once-colorful buttons. Don heard Jack swear under his breath a time or two, but based on the content, they were directed at the damaged controls, not at him.

Scalia pounded the nav station with his fist and shook his head. "Well, I *think* I can set the magnetron from here, but I hope one of you remember which little blue dot in the sky is Earth. 'Cause if we slid off-course when we were hit by whatever we were hit by, the comm dishes sure aren't usin' *this* thing to zero in on home. And forget about chasing Voyager's tail. Nav computer is officially cooked!"

"Bloody hell," spat Bouchard, taking a cue from his wife, "I hadn't even thought of that!" He took a deep breath. "Check out the shuttles, Scales. If either of them is still intact, remotely tie in its nav computer into *Explorer Two's* astrometrics. We need to find out if we are still on-course."

"Roger, Darko," Jack replied, and floated over to another set of screens displaying shuttle status and allowing remote control of each one.

"X-Ray," called Don, "are your comm systems still locked onto Earth?"

"Negative."

The reply had come fast, as if the information was already known. "Negative? But... Ray you've been down there for a good ten minutes! Why didn't you—"

Science Specialist Ray "X-Ray Eyes" Isley's overly-polite voice boomed in the cabin from multiple speakers. "I was waiting until the right time to tell you."

"When you found out would have been a good time," Don replied.

"My apologies, Commander," the android said. "It sounded like you had more important things on your mind at the moment."

"Telling Mission Control what happened and getting some guidance is right up there in the realm of important things on my mind!"

"Yes, Commander."

"Wait," Adrienne interrupted, "Ray, did you turn on our mics? Have you been eavesdropping again?"

"I will notify you as soon as we have a lock, Commander," the metal and plastic man said, ignoring the question. "Once Mr. Scalia ties the navigation system through the communications array, I can recalibrate the system."

"You have!" yelled Pearls. "Ray, we talked about this!"

Silence.

"Thank you, X-Ray," Don concluded.

"You're welcome, Commander."

Adrienne set her jaw. "Oh, he is in so much trouble it's not even funny."

Don smiled. "He's still learning, you know. In a way, he's just a seven-year-old boy. He was all of *one* when we launched."

"A seven year old who's not going to get to play Uno with his favorite pilot tonight! Did you hear that, Ray?"

"Commander!" yelled Jack.

Bouchard's head spun to the forward windows so fast, the motion made his body spin that direction as well in the zero-G. He grabbed a nearby handle and scolded himself for not fastening his seat belt. "Did you see something, Scales?"

"I... I thought I did." He shook his head. "Maybe I was just seeing things?"

"What did you see?" Pearls asked, her large, brown eyes scanning the stars off to the front-right. "Did you see my lasers? Do you believe me now?"

"X-Ray!" shouted Bouchard, before Jack could answer. "Check your backup radar. Anything?"

"I'll need to boot it up, Commander. Give me a few seconds."

"Soon as humanly possible, X-Ray."

"Funny," the android replied from one deck below. "Honestly, Commander, I doubt it will pick up anything. Otherwise, Mister Scalia would have seen it at his station before the initial attack."

"Probably, but let's make sure." A thought occurred to Bouchard. "X-Ray, would we even be able to see an object out here, this far out from the sun?"

"Possibly. For comparison, at Neptune's orbit, thirty Astronomical Units from the sun, the illumination factor is approximately two watts per meter square. At one hundred and twenty-two Astronomical Units from the sun, we might see one watt per meter square of illumination."

"X-Ray," said Bouchard, "country-speak for me, please, like we talked about."

"Oh yes," Ray replied, "again, my apologies. So, at Neptune, the sun illuminates objects close to what you might see on a dark country road with a waxing or waning gibbous moon overhead. Where we currently are, you might see half of that amount of light. If an object is made of a highly-reflective material, yes, you might see it with your human eyes."

"But if it's a ship made with a light-absorbing material, or painted with military camouflage..."

"I understand what you're thinking, Commander. It would appear as black as Mister Liev's Angus bull, and you may only see it when it blocks the stars behind it."

"It was my Pa's bull, not mine," Mag-Lev broke in.

Everybody's dropping eaves it would seem. Bouchard ignored the comment. "Is your radar booted up yet, Ray?"

"The system is running through its final startup diagnostics," the android said. "Twenty-three more seconds."

Bouchard had another fear, but he didn't voice it to the others. He tried hard to bury the idea of an alien vessel boasting a cloaking device into the recesses of his ten-year-old memory, where the warships of old science fiction movies he'd watched with his father still lived. "Adrienne, do you have anything on your short-range?"

"Short-range is as blank as long-range," the pilot replied, motioning to a glowing three-dimensional sphere hovering between them. "But that may not mean it is malfunctioning. It could just mean that whatever is out there is not yet within 300,000 *K* of us."

"If it's not within 300,000 kilometers," said Bouchard, "and yet Jack still saw something moving—"

"I know," she agreed.

"I must have just imagined it," said Jack. "Otherwise it would have to be the size of a small moon."

"That's no moon..." Isley quipped over the comm.

Bouchard sighed. "Always packed full of humor, aren't you, X-Ray?"

"I'm just as God programmed me, sir."

Adrienne rolled her eyes. Apparently the outlandishness of a robot bringing up the concept of a higher deity wasn't lost on her. She cocked her head. "There is another possibility," she said. "Maybe it's like, a stealth craft or something?"

Despite Bouchard's earlier cool logic, the mere mention of the word "craft" by his pilot—alluding to her apparent acceptance of aliens that could build such things—sent a shiver up his spine. He looked up and behind him at Scales, whose fingers were flying across the controls in front of him. Either he hadn't heard Adrienne, or chose to ignore her comment.

"Okay!" Scalia turned toward the others. "I've boosted the magnetic field to one zero-zero-zero, and rerouted the power relays to the mag-field detector, which is now working again. I'm sweeping it in a wide arc in front of us. If something is inside our field of detection, it will return a—"

>Bleep<

Bouchard froze.

The three looked at one another.

"Woah," muttered Pearls, breaking the silence. "Scales, what's the range of that thing?" Her voice was a whisper, as if the thing outside could hear her.

>Bleep<

"I need a distance, Scales," said Bouchard. *Maybe I should be whispering too?*

"Seven hundred and thirty nine kilometers," Jack reported.

>Bleep<

"Now six hundred eighty seven."

Adrienne snapped her head toward the radar, and sighed. "Nothing." She looked up at Bouchard. "I didn't mean to jinx us with the whole stealth thing."

He reached out and patted her on the shoulder. "I'm sure the radar is malfunctioning."

"Long range is just as I feared," Ray interjected, his voice loud in the small space of the command cabin, "it's not picking up anything. However, now that I know the distance of the object thanks to Mr. Scalia's ingenuity, I can manually scan that precise range and zero in on whatever is— Bingo."

"You got something already?" asked Don.

"Spectrographic is returning an echo. High mineral content, various alloys."

"See?" said Scalia. "It *is* an asteroid! Just as—"

"It's no asteroid," Isley corrected. "The object is oddly symmetrical. It looks less like an asteroid and more like a—"

"There it is!" Pearls shouted.

"Where?" asked Bouchard.

"There!" She pointed somewhere off to her left, not to her right, where the three had been looking for aliens previously.

Bouchard squinted and scanned the stars. "I'm sorry, Pearls, I'm not—" Then he saw it. A tiny speck of black occulting one of the myriad stars. Then another. "I see it!" He could follow its path across the sky fairly easily, now that he knew where to look. But a moment later, it didn't blacken the next star like he expected it to do. "Wait, where'd it go?"

"I lost it, too," said Pearls. Then a second later, "There!" she exclaimed.

Bouchard shook his head. "You and your eagle eyes."

"You see it?" Pearl's eyes were intense when she turned to face him. "Did it just perform a course correction? It's like it's going... sideways now."

"Actually, it's moving toward us," said Isley over the speakers.

Bouchard looked back at Scales. "Your asteroid just made a right turn, Navigator."

TWO

Bouchard's heart pounded in his chest. He strapped himself in, because floating out of the seat when you're trying to work is annoying, but floating away when alien visitors could come knocking on your window could be downright embarrassing. "Mags!" His call came out like an eight-year-old girl had just squealed. Bouchard closed his eyes, took a deep breath, and let his shoulders drop. *Try again.* "Mags," he said in his normal voice. "We need every ounce of thrust we can get out of what's left of our ion drive. I'm going to take advantage of our powerplant dishing out a hundred and ten percent, and push those last two engines at a hundred and ten percent. For your detailed repair inspection, enlist Treads. She knows as much as you when it comes to those things. I'm gonna shoot for the moon here; if you can get one or more of the less damaged engines working now, make it happen."

Liev's voice came over the speakers once again. "What's the urgency? Is something else about to hit us? Same thing that hit us earlier? A meteorite or somethin'?"

"No," Bouchard replied. "I think we might have company."

Larry spoke again, but in a softer tone. "Company like, you're givin' personality to inanimate objects, or company like, little green men from Mars?"

"I'm afraid it may be the latter," said Bouchard. He received an earful of silence for a few heartbeats.

"He's joking, right?" That came from his wife. Her voice sounded distant, as if she was being picked up by Mag-Lev's microphone implant rather than her own.

"I wish I was joking, babs. X-Ray, send out the sweetest 'hello' you can muster on all frequencies."

"Wilco," Ray replied.

Now safely seated properly in at the helm, Bouchard saw a flurry of activity to his left. Adrienne had begun a systems check, turning the flight stick across all axes and slamming the throttle forward and backward. She seemed to be willing the controls to execute an escape maneuver. All she accomplished was a slow spin of the star field. "Well, the attitude thrusters work," she said. "But we might as well be batakh sitting pretty for the hunter."

Bouchard smiled. "I think you mean ducks."

She turned to him. "That's what I said."

Don stared at the dark smudge now almost directly in front of them, blocking several stars now that it was closer. "Well we sure as hell can't outrun or outmaneuver them."

"We couldn't even if our fragile little home was in perfect shape," said Pearls. This ship was designed to go in pretty much one direction, not dogfight like a fighter craft."

Don lowered his voice. "What would Captain Jean Luc Picard do..?"

Behind him, Jack sighed. "Darko, you know we don't know nothin' about your French-Canadian war heroes."

Bouchard shook his head. "Uncultured swine."

"You know," Jack continued, running a hand through his jet-black hair, "I'm guessing that thing could make quick work of us considering it zipped in this close before we even saw it coming. Mining lasers likely wouldn't cut it, pardon the pun. And I'm guessing using nukes in a first-contact scenario probably wouldn't be the best way to introduce ourselves."

Pearls gasped. "Oh, no. If they discover those..."

Bouchard took a deep breath. "Hopefully they're advanced enough to realize what they're for."

"Here's to hoping," Jack muttered.

Bouchard turned back to Scalia. "Glad to hear you've joined us on the *E.T. Team*, by the way."

Scales pursed his lips into a tight smile. "When faced with facts..."

Bouchard nodded, then turned to face his station. "Looks like we're still cruising along at just over 210,000 KPH, same as before the attack. Scales, can you tell if they're matching it? And does anybody know yet if we're still on course? My screen here is still returning an error."

"Looks like it," Jack replied. "The speed-matching, I mean. Navigation-wise, your station is still configured to my busted-up nav system. Let me check on the status of Shuttle Two's nav computer. Last I checked, it was still in the process of booting up."

"Roger, Jack."

"Their rate of advancement has slowed drastically," said Pearls. "They seem to be inching up to us. They're sitting currently at just over fifty kilometers out." She looked at Don. "You know what that means, don't you? That means they've got their engines in reverse, and they're still moving faster than we are, and without any help from a planetary gravity assist."

Bouchard sat back and let what she said sink in. *I hadn't even thought of that...*

Adrienne turned to him and spoke softly. "What do you think they're like? Do you think they might really be little green men?"

Don chuckled. "No. I don't have the capacity to guess."

"I'm hoping for squat little guys with glowing hearts and long necks," said Adrienne.

Bouchard narrowed his eyes when she turned to face him.

She smiled. "Hey, you're the one who mentioned E.T."

He nodded. "That I did."

Scalia broke in. "Long as they're not nine feet tall with two mouths and acid for blood, I'd call it a good day."

Bouchard turned towards Pearls and Scales simultaneously. "You both know about every alien from the old films, but you miss almost all my other references. How is that?"

Jack shrugged. "Everybody knows all about aliens and monsters. That's what keeps every kid up at night. Kept me up, anyway."

Don turned back to the cockpit windows, cocked his head to one side, and stared at the alien ship. It now accurately resembled a tiny lump of pitch-black coal, silently edging in their direction. "Maybe they want something?"

The pilot snorted. "What could we possibly offer aliens who have mega-fast stealth craft and laser beams?"

"I don't know. Information? Knowledge of Earth culture? History? Medicine?"

"Live specimens from Earth," offered Ray Isley.

Silence filled the cabin.

"They haven't destroyed the ship," the android continued, "so it logically follows they mean to keep us alive for some strategic, economic, political, or scientific reason."

"As long as it's not to keep their food fresh." This from Scalia.

"Okay, stop." Bouchard shivered. "You're scaring the women."

Adrienne glanced his way.

"Meaning *me*."

Pearls' beautiful white teeth shined brightly again.

"Well," Bouchard continued, "they haven't taken another 'pot shot' at us. Yet. Maybe if we play our cards right we might actually see another day."

"Should I hail them again, Commander?" asked Ray over the speakers.

"Sure, X-Ray, go ahead," Don said. "Matter of fact, just set the preprogrammed greeting to broadcast on an infinite loop. You know, the one we got from NASA that says 'hello' in fifty-eight languages? Perhaps they simply don't speak English?"

"You think?" Scales snipped, with more than a subtle hint of sarcasm in his voice. "Unless they have a universal translator, or have been watching our television broadcasts since the 1950s, we're probably screwed."

"Enough with the sci-fi references, Jack. That's my job."

Adrienne sat up straight. "Even if they don't understand it, maybe they'll get sick of listening to it and decide to respond?"

"Or get sick of listening to it and blow up the thing making all the racket," offered Scalia.

Bouchard gave him a look that said, with no uncertainty, *You're not helping.*

Scales shrugged and turned back to his console.

"Open up VG circuits two through four, Ray. Give us the best chance of getting though."

"Yes, Commander."

"And while we wait for our friends to... do whatever they're going to do, I guess I'd better put together a quick report to Mission Control. While I still can."

"And I'll keep working on a way for you to actually get it to where it's going," said Jack.

"Thanks, Scales." Don opened up a comm window on the screen in front of him and stared at it.

"What are you gonna tell them?" asked Adrienne.

The cursor on the screen blinked again and again, taunting him. "Haven't got that far yet."

* * *

Five minutes later, Adrienne pointed a finger toward the transparent ceramic window in front of her. "Someone tell me those are antennae and not gun turrets."

Bouchard looked up. The speck of coal that had been inching toward them was about the size of his outstretched fist in front of him, and now had a definite shape. But it wasn't one he could have described. It was lumpy in some spots, jagged in others, and looked nothing like a spacecraft in even Hollywood's history. "Well, if you're talking about the spiky things jutting off the midsection there, I don't think those are antennae."

"That's what I was afraid of," Pearls said softly.

"I wonder how many more of those things that aren't antennae are pointed at us?" asked Scalia.

"Okay, I've got a rough draft," Bouchard interrupted. "How does this sound? 'Mission Control, blah blah blah... 7 May, 2177. At approximately 1830 Zulu Time, *Explorer Two* was hit with unknown radiation or possibly projectiles, apparently emitted from a non-natural source. No casualties, four of six ion engines offline, other damage to ship is minor. Commencing repairs. Non-natural source is on intercept course. Will transmit an update in one hour.' And then the usual sign off."

"No mention of our casualty?" asked Perle.

Bouchard's fingers danced on the screen before him. "One... fish..."

"Two fish," said X-Ray. "Red fish..."

"Blue fish," finished Pearls.

Bouchard ignored the playful banter between his pilot and science specialist, and read aloud his edited manuscript. "'One casualty: one male fish in our two deep-space marine reproduction experiments.' There, happy?" He scanned the report once more and then said, "Go ahead and send it, would you please, Mister Isley? They'll get it in, what, fifteen hours at this distance?"

"Closer to sixteen, actually," Ray replied. "I'll send it right away, Commander."

As if in response, the comm circuit crackled. Bouchard jerked his head to his left, to see Adrienne staring at him with wild eyes.

"What was that?" she whispered.

Bouchard's heart quickened. "X-Ray, was that feedback from the VG-1 circuit, or...?"

Ray's voice sounded even and calm. "It's them."

THREE

The alien ship that now filled most of the forward-facing windows of the cabin had appeared to come to a complete stop, but Bouchard knew this wasn't the case. It was backing up at over 210,000 kilometers per hour, and had exactly matched *Explorer Two's* speed and course after their gravity-assist boost at Neptune. The thing seemed close enough to wave hello. So Don Bouchard did just that. No one waved back. Or if they did, he didn't notice it. He couldn't even make out any windows or hatches or much of anything else on the ugly lump of charcoal.

"Does anyone see any windows?" Pearls asked, as if reading his mind.

He studied the alien vessel for a "bridge" or something that might house the people or creatures that commanded the clunky-looking spaceship. Nothing jumped out as an obvious command and control center. It could be buried deep inside, especially if this was a military craft.

Bouchard let out a deep breath. "Perhaps—" He was cut off by a blue light that bathed the command cabin completely. He shaded his eyes from the glare.

"What is that?" Scales asked. "A weapon of some kind?"

Bouchard looked down at himself, then tried to cup the light with his palm to see if it inflicted any pain. "I don't think so. It doesn't hurt or anything."

"They seem to be scanning us with a particle-like beam," explained Ray. "It's engulfing *Explorer Two* in its entirety."

"Right," agreed Adrienne. "It's like when the police come up behind you and shine that bright light in your—" Her eyes became large. "Woah! We're slowing down!"

Bouchard checked the gauges on his console. Sure enough, their speed was decreasing. Soon he felt the forward pull of inertia. Like Pearls was putting on the brakes. But she wasn't. The pull became stronger, and Don was glad he had strapped himself in. He jammed his finger into the ship-wide comms switch. "Everyone hold onto something! We're braking. *Hard!*" As he grabbed a handle off to his right, he heard a clickety-clack sound behind him, which he was sure was Scales scrambling to get into his own restraining harness. *Explorer Two* creaked and groaned around him. Softly at first, then more violently.

Uh oh.

If and when a breaking maneuver was required, the ship was designed for "easy" slow-downs over the course of days or weeks. She wasn't designed for the kinds of G-forces the alien ship was exerting on it now. *Saint Dominic,* Don prayed silently, *hold her together!*

A small notebook flew past Bouchard's head. He heard a cracking sound to his right. His gaze darted in that direction just in time to see a small line appear in the corner of one of the six-inch thick, Fifth-generation Aluminum OxyNitride windows. Bouchard swallowed.

Oh my God.

AlON5 was a polycrystalline transparent ceramic material—"transparent aluminum" to science fiction aficionados—designed to deflect hoards of small meteorites speeding in at up to five hundred thousand kilometers per hour, should any happen to make it through the ship's far-reaching magnetic field. In very public tests back on Earth, a mere one-inch-thick sheet of AlON5 deflected a cannon ball, a tank round, and a missile fired at it. Don had chuckled at the time; as powerful as those projectiles traditionally were, they amounted to not even $1/100^{th}$ of the sheer speed of objects *Explorer Two* might experience beyond the orbits of the dwarf planets Pluto, Eris, Haumea, and Makemake. Not to mention the other three-dozen known objects roughly the same size of Pluto that orbited the sun out past Neptune, most of which had been detected or verified by Ray Isley and *Explorer Two's* telescopes over the last two or three years. But such displays made the general public—which understood little to nothing of such things—feel good about the safety of Bouchard's crew, who had a whopping six inches of the miracle material between them and the evils of outer space. The cockpit windows were arguably some of the strongest "walls" on the entire ship, hence why they were allowed to be so big and nearly wrap all the way around the command cabin.

And one had just cracked.

Bouchard realized then why the entire ship wasn't made of the stuff, like he and the crew had often joked. Its windows aside, the *Explorer Two*, mighty as it was to make it all the way to the edge of interstellar space, would have been barely stronger than aluminum foil and tissue paper in the atmosphere of Earth. The alien ship bearing down didn't need Buck Rogers-style "laser guns" to destroy her; she would be crushed with nothing but inertia.

Can't the newcomers see we are falling apart?

A loud bang came from Adrienne's side of the cockpit, and a crack spread halfway across the window before her. Red lights sparked to life all across the console in front of them, and alarms blared.

This is it, thought Don. *We made it eleven billion miles from home, but this is the end of the road. Will the aliens recover our mutilated bodies? Or simply fly off, their job complete? Will future astronauts be allowed to retrieve us? Should such a mission even be attempted? Because the same thing might happen to anyone who—*

A voice over the comm system interrupted his macabre thoughts. Bouchard froze and stared at the alien ship. Was it his imagination? The chaos around him was deafening, and he couldn't tell. Until he heard it again.

It began as jibberish. Clicks, chirps, groans, growls. Then a word he recognized.

"STOP."

He looked at his crewmates. "Did you guys hear that?" he shouted over the din.

"I heard it," yelled Scalia.

What did it mean? *Is the voice telling us to stop? Why, when the blue light is doing a good job of that already?* Or could it possibly be, Bouchard dared to dream, the alien captain telling his crew to stop, because they realized *Explorer Two* couldn't handle the stress? On cue, the light surrounding the ship dimmed, then winked out. The violent groans ceased, as did most of the forward tug on his body, but the creaking and the alarms continued.

"Did they finally figure out they were about to rip us apart!?" asked Scales.

"Let's hope so!" Bouchard replied over the squealing alarms. He looked down at his station. The ship's speedometer read 94,672.34 kilometers per hour. "Let's get these alarms shut down!" he hollered at the others. He silenced as many as he could at his station, and saw Pearls and Scalia doing the same, but the chaos continued. "Bypass what you can! Switch on all auxiliaries!" Don threw switches and heard others around him being thrown, which had the effect of finally quelling the klaxon, and turning some of the red flashing lights green or amber. The cabin now quieter, he could speak in a normal voice again. "Let's hope we didn't lose any air."

More sounds came across the open comm channel. One was an unmistakable but raspy order. It said simply, "GO."

Don held his breath.

"Was that them?" Adrienne asked.

Bouchard looked her way. "That wasn't the voice of anyone on *this* ship."

"Go?" she asked. "Does that mean they want us to leave?"

Another English word followed in the same raspy, scratchy voice. "EARTH." Then more chirping sounds. Then silence.

"Well, I don't know about you two," said Scalia, "but the message is pretty clear to me."

Bouchard nodded. "You may be right, Scales. But if they're expecting us to return to Earth, they're in for a disappointment." With a mere thought, he activated the microphone on the implant near his ear. "Mag-Lev. Any luck with that ion drive?"

"Not yet, boss," came the reply. "We've barely even assessed the damage. Hey, what's going on up there? Are you done tearin' up the ship? What just came over the comm system? Was that a garbled communique from Houston?"

"Unfortunately not. I suspect it was an order from our new 'friends'. One I can't follow even if I wanted to." He addressed his science specialist. "Patch me in to their frequency, X-Ray."

"Done," Ray announced over the loudspeaker. "You're on."

This was it. The moment Bouchard had dreamed of nearly his entire life, but never thought might actually happen. *Stick to the script,* he told himself. *This will go down in the history books just like Neil Armstrong's first words from the Moon, Elwin Ransom's when he stepped foot on Mars, and Rupert Chang's broadcast from the icy surface of Europa.* Don took a deep breath. "Greetings! My name is Commander Don Bouchard, in command of the International Spaceship *Explorer Two.* We are peaceful explorers from the planet Earth!" He paused then, so as not to overwhelm whoever may be listening. "I am pleased to meet you, and hope my people and yours can live in harmony, and benefit from a peaceful sharing of knowledge." He then waited for a response.

None came.

He waited some more.

"Did they hear us?" Adrienne asked.

"I've boosted the signal, Commander," announced X-Ray. "I've also spread the frequencies as far across the radio spectrum as I can. We're now broadcasting from thirty Hertz up to thirty GigaHertz. Please try again."

"Okay." Bouchard raised his voice. "Greetings. We are peaceful explorers from Earth. My name is Commander Don Bouchard, in command of—"

Gurgles and clicks and chirps cut him off. Then came the English words again, which sounded like a scream across course sandpaper. "GO. EARTH." Then the cabin was quiet once again.

Bouchard looked over at Pearls, who was staring at him with a face that appeared frozen in time. He turned back to the lump of coal, swearing to himself that he would not be scared off so easily. "Alien vessel. This is Commander Don Bouchard, we would like to meet you. This is an historic occasion for us. Our people have never met any—"

"GO!" the voice repeated. Then a new word followed. "NOW."

Bouchard sighed and looked around at the others. Every eye was on him. "I understand you, sir. But we cannot go back to Earth. Our engines have been damaged by your weapons. We need time to enact repairs." He thought adding the fact they would need to perform a 180-degree spin, plus request a boost toward the sun, would add too much to the conversation at this point.

More strange noises came then, from what sounded like multiple creatures. Bouchard listened with fevered intent. *Do they understand?*

"Sounds like they're arguing," said Adrienne.

Scalia added, "Probably about whether or not to help us or kill us."

"Let's hope it's the former," Bouchard said, and leaned back in his seat.

"You guys are so calm," said Perle. "I'm totally freaked out over here!"

"Pearls, calm down." Bouchard reached over and grabbed her hand. It shook in his. *She's serious.* "Adrienne, it'll be okay. I need my pilot right now. Okay? Adrienne?"

She looked up. Her eyes glistened.

"Adrienne, I know you're scared. You don't think I'm scared? Look at me, my hands are shaking, too."

She looked down. "No they're not."

"Well, that one's not." He held up his right hand and shook it all over the place. "But I run the ship with this hand!"

This made her giggle.

"Look at Scales. You don't think he's scared?"

"I pissed my pants," the man behind them admitted.

Bouchard hoped he was joking, but he honestly couldn't tell. "See?"

Now smiling, she nodded. "I'll be okay, Donnie. It's just that... these are *aliens*. Real, Honest-to-Rama aliens. Not the kind from the movies. Not puppets or human beings in costumes or created in a computer. These are intelligent creatures from another world! I... I'm sorry, I'm just..." Her voice trailed off.

"I know," Bouchard said. "As soon as I have time to process all of this, I'm sure I'll be right there with—"

Low gurgling sounds came from the speakers again. Then chirping. The chirping—no, squawking—seemed to be a new voice. Bouchard thought he heard the word "Wait" in there somewhere. He looked at his pilot. She stared back at him.

A thought occurred to Bouchard. "Oh man, what was I thinking?"

"What?" Pearls yelled.

Bouchard punched a button. "X-Ray! We need to be taking photos, holos!"

"Already on it, Commander," Ray replied. "I started nineteen minutes ago, when the alien ship was first within visual distance. I'm capturing images across the visual spectrum. I've also got our spectrometers, photometers and interferometers trained on it."

I should have known. "Good. I think we should—"

The word "WAIT" boomed across the loudspeakers, then the channel fell silent again.

Bouchard stared at the ugly alien lump for a moment, then looked to his two bridge companions. "Well," he said, "I'm guessing it would be pointless to ask for how long."

No one smiled.

"Alright then, I'm going to take this opportunity to get below, check on the repairs and the status of my crew. Not to mention my wife, who I'm sure is itching for an explanation."

"I'm sure she's pieced the puzzle together by now," Jack said. "She's quite the clever lass."

"I'm sure you're right." Bouchard patted Adrienne on the back on his way toward the hatch at the rear of the cabin. He paused on his way out the door and turned back. "Pearls? Keep an eye on that thing. If it so much as blinks, call me on the spot."

"Absolutely, boss."

FOUR

Bouchard floated through the only door to the command cabin and tossed his body down a white, vertical shaft. It was large enough to allow two people to pass each other going opposite directions, which was truly a luxury in the world of economical spacecraft. He used one of the two ladders running along opposite walls of every one of these types of shafts scattered throughout the ship. He and the crew had learned early on to be careful; it was easy to lose control of your trajectory with haphazard "zipping" along these corridors, not to mention the severe difficulty when it came to stopping yourself should you encounter another crewman.

Ahead of him lay intersections to decks two and three, all brightly lit and as white as a hospital room. The entire ship was white, in fact, inside and out. Thankfully, Don decided, it didn't smell like a hospital. *Explorer Two* boasted mainly the smell of plastic, rubber, lubricant, canvas, and occasionally, dinner. *The smell of home,* he thought. Thankfully, it didn't smell too much like "space." To Don, when he returned from a spacewalk in Earth orbit, his suit had an acrid, sulfuric smell, like a combination of hot metal, welding fumes, and a steak that had just been seared on the grill. Even out here, doing spacewalks in the depths of the solar system, it wasn't much different. He still didn't know what it was from. Atomic oxygen clinging to the material? High energy ions? *X-Ray will know.*

He stopped at Junction Number Two and floated into the Science and Astronomy cabin, located directly below the command cabin. Since the windows—equally as large and numerous as those surrounding the command cabin one deck up—were currently covered by their external shutters, it would have been pitch-black were it not for sixteen illuminated screens situated in a horseshoe-like array around the lone silhouette of a man. The man's outstretched arms moved from one screen to the next, his fingers dancing on their surfaces like a musician strumming delicate, glowing harps. Bouchard floated up behind him. "So X-Ray, you find anything interesting?"

Ray Isley turned his head and smiled. "I've discovered entire textbooks worth of interesting data on our new friends, Commander. Most of it likely of more interest to myself and scientists back on Earth than to you and the others."

"Humor me."

"Alright." The android rotated his body to face the series of screens to Don's right. Most of them showed various parts of the exterior of the ship, but some showed the alien vessel in various visuals. Ray drew Don's attention to one in particular, and pointed to illuminated patches on the nearly black, spiky blob, which Bouchard recognized as the alien ship. "As you can see in this thermal image," Ray began, "these red and yellow locations show hotspots, but they aren't thrusters. The reverse and attitude thrusters are located here and here. As you can see, they are all quite cold."

Don shook his head. "But they were probably shut down now that they've matched our speed. It's understandable they're not emitting heat now."

"This isn't a live feed, sir," said Ray, "this video was taken eleven minutes ago, before their particle beam slowed us down. At the time I recorded this, the alien ship was still attempting to match our speed, which at the time was 211,397.6 KPH, which means they had to be using thrusters located on the side of the vessel that, as far as I can tell, has always been facing us. Whatever they are using for thrust, it isn't a chemical reaction, a nuclear reaction, an ion engine, an Electro-Mechanical drive, nor any other traditional, non-theoretical propulsion I am familiar with."

"Interesting."

"Quite. The hotspots are very intriguing," continued Ray. "I suspect they are vents on the outer hull, releasing excess heat generated by the ship's power source. Whatever that may be."

Bouchard grabbed a nearby hold so as not to float into a wall. "Those aren't showing hot spots on the inside of the ship? I simply assumed—"

"I haven't been able to penetrate the inside of the vessel, Commander."

"Really," Don said, more as a statement than a question. "Not even your eyes can see through it, huh?"

The android's expression didn't change.

Oh you can tell jokes, but when I try... Don let it go. "Have you tried the Dense-Body Penetrating—"

"Yes," Ray interrupted. "And every other radar and sensor *Explorer Two* has. That ship is either made from material more dense than four kilometers of osmium, or the walls are lined with some alloy or synthetic material I'm—again—not familiar with."

Don nodded. "Well, they are aliens, after all. They might have gadgets and gizmos as far ahead of us as we have compared with Lewis and Clark."

"Ah," replied Ray, "explorers from the Nineteenth Century. I had to access my library for that one. Very clever. And I agree. It's making my task of collecting data on the alien ship very intriguing, but very frustrating at the same time."

Bouchard nodded. He was sure Ray wasn't frustrated in the same sense that a human being could be; the machine had likely used the word to convey the fact that the trouble he was experiencing would surely frustrate a human.

Sometimes Bouchard had difficulty remembering this near-perfect looking Ivy League candidate, with his full head of luscious blonde hair, wasn't a real person. He looked, moved, and acted exactly like everyone else on board. All the way down to the hairs and blemishes of his warm skin, and the unwelcome puns and practical jokes he pulled when the humans were least expecting it. The engineers had almost made him *too much* like a human. But his nickname was "X-Ray" to remind everyone he most definitely was not; no one else aboard could see through walls. "Anything else?" Don asked. He was itching to get to the Living, Working, and Recreation ring to start his inspection.

"One other thing." Ray touched a series of virtual buttons on one screen, and the image changed on another screen to his right. "I reviewed the visual astrometric data prior to the initial attack. I now know what to look for in terms of detecting another "invisible" vessel that might be heading our way. I thought you might not want to be sneaked up on again."

"You thought right."

Ray nodded. "To that end, it didn't take me long to discover several small, dark shapes all around us that occasionally block the background stars."

Ray's heart skipped a beat. "Several?"

"Nine, in fact. They are not moving towards us, but rather parallel to our trajectory. I postulate they are additional alien vessels observing our encounter."

A chill ran up Bouchard's back.

"There's no telling how long they have been shadowing us," Ray continued. "Like the one parked just outside, they do not show up on radar, either."

"Understood. Okay, well, keep an eye on them. Let me know if any of them decide to join the party."

"Will do, Commander."

Don patted the android on the back—a human gesture, but one he was sure the machine would interpret correctly—and made his way out of the science cabin. *Great. Should have known all those old movies had it right all along.* He paused at the junction of deck three. *Damn.* He had forgotten to ask Ray about the smell. *Oh well, plenty of time to ask later.*

FIVE

Deck three of *Explorer Two* was the longest tunnel on the entire ship. It ran from the bow all the way to the protective shield, three hundred meters—over three American Football fields—down the length of the one thousand meter vessel. From it, a crewmember could access every location on his or her wayward abode. Namely—in order of opportunity from stem to stern—the large maintenance bay directly below Science and Astronomy (from whence Don had just come), the tunnel leading up to the command cabin and Science and Astronomy, the Living, Working, and Recreational, or "LWR" ring, the observation towers, the magnetron that provided their protective magnetic field, the two shuttles—one docked to port and the other to starboard—and the numerous storage bins carrying materials used by the ship's 3D printers to create most tools and repair parts the crew needed on their voyage. They could also use the materials to print food and morale items if desired, so long as unnecessary items were recycled after use like everything else. Don still couldn't figure out how he was going to get Jack to recycle the guitar he printed up in the first month of their voyage, nor the espresso machine Adrienne threatened to kill anyone who touched, but he would find something to hold over their heads eventually.

The towers. He could restrict Pearls use of them. But could he be so mean? The observation towers were Pearls' favorite hang-out; it was no wonder she was there when the incident occurred. Tower One shot three hundred meters straight "up", and Tower Two led the same distance straight "down", each with an AlON5 ceramic-glass sphere at its peak. A person could see the entire ship from either the one above or below the vessel. Adrienne would strap herself in up in Tower One and sit for hours amongst the ferns and flowers, reading just by the starlight from a seemingly infinite number of suns and galaxies. Countless unimaginably luminous objects which the average person could never see merely by looking up from the surface of the Earth. Out here, Don thought, over one hundred times further away from the sun as Earth normally is, there was no atmosphere to filter or twinkle the stars, no cities to wash out their gentle light. Not even a dark boat at the center of the Pacific Ocean could reveal the view Bouchard and his crew enjoyed every single "day." It was one of the few "pros" he counted against the bucketful of "cons" of participating on this mission, the biggest con being the fact he nor any of his crew would ever see the Pacific Ocean ever again.

Don pushed off various handholds until he reached the hub of the LWR ring. The ring was only place on the ship with something resembling gravity, hence the reason they mainly lived, worked, and "recreated" there. It was centripetal force, not exactly real gravity, but it was the best option they had to keep their bones from degrading in zero-G. It was an idea that had been in science fiction novels for at least two hundred years, but it was still the best alternative the top scientific minds of Earth could come up with, short of hijacking an asteroid bigger than the Moon and using it as a spaceship.

The ring was a work of art in itself. The spheres "atop" the two towers had to be six hundred meters apart in order to clear the five hundred meter-wide rotating wagon wheel that was the LWR ring. The thing had to be a particular minimum size so that the crew—who had to live in it quite literally the rest of their lives—wouldn't suffer ill effects, things most people living on Earth had never experienced and would never dream about. Don grasped the concepts, if not the math involved with things like "gravity gradient", where perceived gravity at your head was different than at your feet. Or when a high angular velocity could create "cross-coupling", where simply turning your head in the conduct of a normal day's duties could cause motion sickness and dizziness. Then there was tangential velocity, which had to be maximized in order to reduce the Coriolis Effect, which can distort your apparent gravity. If this is too low, people become disoriented when simply walking around. All these things add up a ridiculously large—and ridiculously expensive—space wagon wheel, indeed.

Bouchard maneuvered into the hub—a white, spherical room which rotated around him. He grabbed a nearby handhold, and was gently jerked into the same "perspective" as the ring. Now the long tunnel he had just left appeared to be rotating instead of the hub.

Sharing the room with him were four pillars, each housing an elevator leading in four different directions, and alongside each of these were emergency ladders shafts leading "down" to the floors of the inner and outer rings. Don used his wristwatch to call his wife. Last they spoke she was in Auxiliary Command and Control. "Brea? Are you still in the ACC?"

"Still here, dear," she replied. "Are you coming down?"

"Be there in a jiffy."

As the elevator "dropped", he felt the ever-increasing but welcome pull of the false gravity, not unlike being on a carnival ride. By the time his boot touched the floor of the inner ring, one hundred twenty-five meters "down", the tangential velocity was just under twenty-five meters per second, and the angular velocity was a comfortable two rotations per minute. His insides had all fallen back into place once again, even though he only experienced one-half Earth gravity here in this inner ring. He was heavy compared to what he had been only a few seconds earlier, but the illusion of weight felt good.

The inner ring housed all the experimental lab, as well as the technical science and engineering stations. The outer ring, another one hundred and twenty-five meters further down, was where Don's body was almost fully tricked into believing normal

Earth gravity was present, and is where he slept, ate, took a shower, used the latrine, saw the doc, and made love to his wife. On that ring, the angular velocity remained the same—1.89 rotations per minute—but the tangential velocity had increased to almost fifty. Whatever that meant; Bouchard could have cared less. He only cared that he and Brea wouldn't hurt themselves when they crawled into bed.

Occasionally he wondered if he would ever get the hang of zero-G sex. Occasionally he wondered if Brea would ever allow him to try again.

The three couples on board had given up experimenting with the novelty early on in the mission after ending up with cuts, bruises, and in the case of Pearls and Mag-Lev, a minor concussion.

Don bounded up to his wife in the half-gravity, not unlike astronauts bounced on the surface of the moon. He had to be careful lest he bump his head. *Again.* Treads was busy at a wall of screens, each with small images of perfectly round bubbles. Several bubbles still silently flashed amber and red, indicating the status of various on-board systems or equipment. He placed gentle hands on her shoulders, covering up the Space X patch on one shoulder, and the British flag on the other. He kissed her large but neatly shaped blonde bun.

She spun around and, without even looking at his face, gave him a tight hug and didn't release it.

"Oh, Brea-baby, it's okay," he whispered, wrapping his arms around her. "We'll be alright. We'll make it out of this."

"Will we?"

"These... people, beings, creatures... they want something, or they would have taken us out long before we ever even saw them."

"But what do they want?" she asked, breaking their embrace. "Are they really... *aliens?*"

"Well, I seriously doubt they're Chinese, unless the new Emperor has been keeping some serious secrets from NASA!"

Treads looked up into his eyes. "But what could we possibly offer people who are advanced enough to be out here ahead of us?"

"I don't know, sweetie. I don't know. Maybe they don't want anything more than for us to go home. You heard them, didn't you? They keep saying 'Go', 'Earth'. And 'Now'! So they may simply want us to turn back. Of course, we all know that's a complete impossibility, unless Planet X or Nibiru really does exist and we can A, find it, and B, reach it, and then somehow sling-shot around and head back toward the Sun. I didn't exactly get a chance to tell our new friends all this, so I hope they don't get too upset when I do."

"I heard them." Brea said quietly. She turned and took a few steps away. "I heard them over the speaker. I just didn't want to believe they're real."

"Yeah, Scales had a hard time with it as well. But he came around."

"I was really hoping this was all just some elaborate training exercise NASA had told you about from the start, and you just didn't tell me or anyone else about it. To really put us to the test and all that."

Bouchard said nothing.

She spun round. "Is it a test?"

Don stared at her for a moment, wondering if he should lie just to keep her from worrying. He decided against it, and shook his head once.

Treads let loose a sigh of exasperation and threw her hands into the air. "I just don't know what to think, Donnie. I don't!" She dropped her arms to her side once again. "This is easier for you. You've been watching all those ridiculous movies all your life."

"They don't seem so silly anymore, do they?"

The sound she made seemed to be a mixture of humor and anger. "Yeah, well. They're all so campy and far-fetched! All the science is wrong."

"Not all of it."

"Most of it. I can't get past it."

"You can't get over the bad science, but the magic in Greek and Roman Mythology doesn't bother you?"

She shrugged. "It's different. It's romantic. And by that I mean heroic, adventurous, mysterious, not—"

"I know what you mean. And I'm not talking about the super-silly films. You simply don't understand the sci fi I enjoy. It's the human experience that really mattered in the early days of science fiction. Not the science. Or lack thereof." Bouchard looked around the room they were in, with its curved floor and ceiling. "And like I said, it wasn't all wrong. I can show you several films that you would swear were filmed right here in this room." He took his wife's hand. "Those old holofilms and books got me where I am today. What's your excuse?"

She chuckled, and ran her fingers gently across his bald head, stopping at his bare neck. "You."

He leaned in and kissed her on the forehead. "We'll be okay. Don't worry, Brea-baby. These aliens seem a little more reasonable than those in 'Independence Day'."

"In what?"

"Nevermind." He smiled. "So where are we on the engineering front?"

"Well," she said, crossing her arms, "Mags and I have rerouted all power and xenon to the two remaining ion arrays. I had to reroute a system or two to get the ACC station back to operational; something must have shorted out somewhere, gotta find that later. But you got your backup, um, back up, and we can fly the ship from here if necessary."

"Good job, as usual."

"Thanks, pet. So! All that's left now is suiting up and dragging our asses outside. Get eyes and hands-on our problem, better than what the mounted camera views can tell us."

"Understood." He took a deep breath. "Alright, well, much as I don't want to say this—what with aliens lurking about outside and all—we'd better get out there and get started."

She nodded. "Roger. I'll get Mags on the horn."

Before she could get away, he took her face in his hands. "You be careful out there, okay?"

She put her hands on top of his and looked up at him with those amazing, crystal-blue eyes that he could swear were real. "I'll start when *you* start."

He seared that beautiful face into his memory, memorized every line, the vector of every eyelash. On one hand there was no need to do so; he had memorized all these features a full decade ago. But today he was worried. For the first time since they had launched six years and three months ago, there was a slight chance that he may never see that face again. "I love you," he whispered.

"I know."

Their inside joke always made Don smile, moreso because he was happy she actually knew *one* ancient science fiction reference. Possibly the most important one of all.

They shared a quick kiss, then Brea tilted her head in an odd way. "Mags? Treads here. Please meet me in Airlock Four in ten minutes. We've just been given the 'Go' for EVA."

"Roger dodger," came the voice of the Mission Specialist over the tiny speaker in Don's implant. Each member of the crew had an identical one behind the ear of his or her choice.

Don received a pat on the butt as Brea strutted past him on her way to the elevator. He watched intently as her shapely hips swayed from side to side as she sauntered to the automatic doors. She wore the same royal-blue NASA one-piece they all did, but somehow, she wore it better than anyone else on board. And she still stirred those feelings deep inside him, the ones he felt when he first laid eyes on her all those years ago.

She turned and blew him one last kiss before the doors closed and she was gone.

"How does she do that?" he asked out loud to himself. Bouchard shook his head to clear it, and continued his inspection.

He walked along the curved floor until he reached another elevator, next to which was a stair that wound around it. Unlike the four primary elevators which connected both rings all the way to the hub, this one, and three others like it, only traveled between the inner ring and outer ring. All the elevators were fast, and in seconds he was at full gravity, 9.8 meters per second, relishing that wonderful fifty meters per second of tangential velocity. Here he walked comfortably just as he would on Earth, and strutted toward *Explorer Two's* Med Lab.

Like all the doors on the ship, he had to open the door to the lab manually. No luxurious automatic sliding doors on this boat, Don mused. He considered himself and his crew lucky they had automatic "lifts", and didn't have to climb hundreds of meters of ladders multiple times a day. Occasionally he and Brea took the ladders and stairs just for fun. Or what Brea called "fun", anyway.

Inside the lab Bouchard found Melodi Meng-Scalia replacing loose items back into their proper places. "Hey there, M&M."

She gasped, spun 'round, and instantly relaxed. "You scared me, Darko!" she said, her almond-shaped eyes giving him a glare.

"Sorry. You okay?"

"I'm fine. Just a little jumpy. All this time in the black has made us pretty complacent, huh? Never would have thought anyone else would be out here!"

"Yeah. A lot of people back on Earth are going to be saying 'told ya so' for the rest of their lives, and lot more are going to be re-examining their place in the universe."

"And probably going to church a lot more," the spritely doctor added, pushing her glasses up on her nose. "Or a lot less, depending..." She giggled like a schoolgirl as she arranged some equipment, in stark contrast to how Don pictured someone holding doctorates in biology, physiology, and medicine would act.

He glanced around and saw a lot of debris lying about. "Looks like an earthquake hit this place." He knelt down and started picking up boxes of gauze and other small items strewn across the floor.

"It kinda did!" The tiny woman's back was now to him. Her long black hair bounced normally here, unlike the slow motion in which it appeared to be in all other parts of the ship. "You just get used to things staying where you left them here in the ring, and then, boom! One little bump, and everything's everywhere!" She closed a cabinet door and turned in his direction. "What happened anyw—Hey, stop that!"

"What?" he asked from a kneeling position. "Just trying to help."

"I've got this, Commander, you've got more important things to worry about!"

Don handed her what he had picked up, and she began putting each item in its proper place. "Okay," he said, "But let me help you get the imaging—"

"No, no, no!" Melodi shook her head violently. "I have the McCoys to help with that heavy thing!" She motioned to the two surgical robots that appeared to be sleeping in their alcoves in one wall.

Sleeping? Or waiting for the right moment to attack? Bouchard hadn't yet decided which. "But those guys—"

"Are very helpful," she interrupted before he could express his mistrust like he often did. "Don't worry, I hid their claw attachments where they can't find them. Their delicate surgical finger attachments could barely snap a stick, let alone your neck. Now get along! Put the ship back together. Let the doctor take care of her office!"

Don raised his eyebrows. "Yes, ma'am!" He stood up, but slowly. Even with all the fancy know-how and velocity calculations that went into their beloved wagon wheel ring design, a person could still get vertigo, even after spending years getting used to the centripedal motion effect. While the ring's spin kept everything stuck to the outer wall—which the crew called the "floor"—Don's pituitary gland often picked up the motion of the cylinder. He had gotten used to it and therefore didn't get motion sickness or dizzy spells, at least not until he over-did it with sudden movement. At which time he was reminded once again that the weight he was so fond of wasn't due to *real* gravity. So he tended to take it easy when the situation allowed.

This was not one of those times.

His hesitation was misinterpreted by Melodi, who was now pushing him toward the door. Apparently he wasn't moving fast enough for her.

Don had forgotten how mighty she was, her little hands unrelenting. "Okay, okay, I'm going!" He stumbled over the threshold as he passed through the doorway.

"Bye!" She smiled, and shut the door in his face.

He jerked his head back just in the nick of time. "Good thing I'm not Pinocchio!" he called through the door, touching his nose to ensure it was still there. Don sighed, and continued his inspection.

As he wandered from room to room, he found himself wondering just what the future now held. Their mission had been of a one-way nature from the start, so since they had never planned on seeing Earth again anyway, what could the aliens really do to them besides torture them or kill them outright?

Well, he thought, *they could torture us. Or kill us outright.*

Bouchard had planned on finally passing on from old age—one hundred twenty years on average these days—close to the utmost inner edge of where it was believed the Oort Cloud might begin. His goal was to make it exactly four thousand AU from the sun before buying the farm. He chuckled to himself that he might have made it too, were it not for these meddling aliens. "Hmm. Maybe Brea's right," he said aloud to himself once again, "I probably watched *way* too many old holos as a kid."

Bouchard did some quick calculations in his head. He found that, even if Mag-Lev could repair the engines to tip-top shape, and assuming they didn't run out of xenon gas, it would take them several years just to get back up to the speed at which they'd been traveling before the aliens attacked. Then another couple of decades after that to reach the 900,000 kilometers per hour they would need to get out to four thousand AU in his lifetime. Their ion engines simply couldn't physically accelerate them any faster, nor pass the 900,000 kilometer per hour speed limit. If *Explorer Two's* propulsion system remained reduced by two-thirds, they would fall far short of his goal by the time he "bought the farm." With only two engines providing thrust, there simply wasn't enough time for the slow acceleration of their bulky home to get "up to speed", so to speak. While their engines were some of the most efficient propulsion machines ever created, they were not the most powerful. Especially when the thing they were pushing weighed-in at just over one hundred and sixty tons.

He shook his head. "Figures."

He checked a thick pane of AlON5 embedded in one wall for cracks. Finding none, he looked outside. In the bright light of the hall, he could see little a slight spackling of stars as they moved slowly past the window. They weren't moving, of course, the ring rotated and made them appear to move. He saw no aliens, but then their ships were likely too small and too dark to be seen from this distance.

As he moved on, Don thought about how this incident would affect their mission. Or if they would even be allowed to continue traveling outward at all.

The crew of *Explorer Two* was hoping to pick up Voyager on radar sometime in the next year, out past the Heliopause, where the Sun's solar wind is overcome by the interstellar medium, and interstellar space truly begins. In another year and a half by their original calculations, they would have used their attitude thrusters to spin *Explorer Two* around to face Earth, and used their main engines to slow the ship down to around fifty-five thousand kilometers per hour. That was the approximate last-known speed of the ancient little probe when Earth's Deep Space Network had finally lost contact with it in 2027. They would refine their data once they had the little probe in their sights, and Jack and Ray could calculate exact numbers.

Once at the target speed—only a hair faster than Voyager 2 was travelling—Bouchard and his team would then spin the ship back around to face the wayward craft, and ever-so-carefully shimmy up right behind it. Upon matching its speed exactly, robot arms would then "flip" the probe onto its back, and caress it into their large maintenance bay, all of which was designed specifically for it.

Now inside the ship, Mags and Treads, surely with the help of X-Ray who would probably never leave its side, would physically grab Voyager and lower it to the deck, its dish facing up. They could then take all the time needed to conduct repairs, refueling, and upgrades.

When those were completed, the plan was then to lift the probe off the floor—where it would float in the zero-G of the bay—and then Pearls would simply drop *Explorer Two's* speed using reverse thrusters. The Voyager craft would eventually drift back "outside", never once losing its initial velocity over the entire adventure.

It would take patience for it to clear the bay, probably a couple of weeks. At that time, robotic arms, controlled by the ship's computer, would again flip Voyager, this time back to its original orientation, its dish and antennae pointing once again towards Earth. When *Explorer Two* was far enough back from the ancient spacecraft, Pearls could fire maneuvering thrusters, and "peel off" onto a new trajectory.

Voyager 2 would be tested, of course, before Bouchard and crew would leave it to its own devices. Most of its systems would be booted up while still in the *Explorer's* hangar bay. Once the probe had a clear line-of-sight with Earth, verification signals to and from would commence. Don would only say his final farewells to this famous little machine he had gotten to know so well over the last decade when he was certain it was alive, healthy, and ready to explore the galaxy with new hope and vigor.

Finally, *Explorer Two's* ion thrusters would be lit again, never to be shut down until she reaches maximum speed, or all her xenon gas is depleted.

She would zoom onward towards whatever its destiny might be, maxing out at around 900,000 Kilometers per hour. Eventually, after allowing for acceleration from approximately 55,000 KPH to 900,000 KPH—which would take a couple of decades to reach—the ship would carry its crew fifty-one AU from the sun every single year. At that rate, Don figured he might see the four thousand AU mark in only ninety-eight more years. He would be the ripe old age of one hundred thirty-six.

Right on schedule.

That was the overall concept anyway. Sounded great on paper, Don thought. And they practiced the Voyager capture-and-release at least a hundred times in simulation before leaving Earth. But he didn't count on things going as smoothly upon practical application. He hoped he was wrong.

He hoped they would still get to find out.

With their upgrades, Voyager 2 should last several hundred more years before needing additional maintenance, as it continued on its own endless journey. Endless as far as the human mind was concerned, anyway.

Voyager 2's next destination, assuming the craft could avoid all astronomical objects that may fall into its path, was long ago calculated to be the stellar neighborhood of Ross 248, a small, red dwarf that is in fact hurtling toward our own solar system. In approximately 37,000 years, the star will more accurately rendezvous with Voyager, rather than the spacecraft travel outward to meet it! After that relatively close encounter of only a couple of light years, the probe will zoom toward the brightest star in Earth's sky, Sirius, passing within five light years of that sun. In approximately 296,000 years.

In the meantime, as propulsion concepts eventually improve to the point where astronauts can fly circles around Voyager 2 in the next century or two, the small relic would have no real need to relay new data back to Earth beyond mere nostalgic purposes. Thus additional maintenance would probably never be required after Bouchard and his crew conduct their refit. In fact, in the days leading up to *Explorer Two's* launch, news commentators postulated that one day in the coming centuries, tourists would be able to zip right up to both Voyagers, as well as Pioneers 1 and 2, New Horizons, Deep Journey, and even Explorer One, and marvel at the little curiosities of the early days of space exploration. Maybe they will even tune-in on their personal implants and listen to "the sounds of space" still being broadcast as a novelty some future entrepreneur can sell to the masses. Then they will fly off again on their way to work or play in one of thousands of as-yet unheard-of solar systems.

Don surmised that *Explorer Two* would by then be considered a museum piece as well, perhaps a memorial, a tomb for him and his wife and the rest of the crew. He could see Ray Isley still holding down the fort, so to speak, and greeting visitors every few years as they stopped by to marvel at the quaint vessel, by then useless to all but space historians and elementary school teachers.

Now at the other side of the LWR ring, near his and Brea's quarters, he considered popping in and seeing what damage had been done to the forest puzzle he and she had been working on these last five weeks. But instead he examined another AlON5 porthole for cracks. Luckily, this one seemed fully intact as well. Soon his focus shifted from looking *at* the metal glass to *through* it. As he stared out at the black nothingness, he laughed at himself. It wasn't like he and his crew were forced to pull over into a weigh station for inspection before continuing down the highway. They had just made first contact with intelligent beings not of Earth! And here he was, worried about getting back on schedule to make his date with a long-lost, two hundred-year-old toy and a bunch of "dirty snowballs", as comets were often called. As far as mission success went, he could call this one "smashing." They could all go home right this very minute and be heralded as heroes, without ever even having truly left the solar system at all.

He shook his head and smiled nervously as he tried to wrap his head around the gravity of it all. "We just discovered aliens!" he said to the walls around him. "But what if they're the kind the late, great Stephen Hawking warned us about? And we just unzipped our proverbial flies and gave them a breadcrumb trail right back home?"

As if hit with a sledgehammer, Don wasn't all that concerned with Voyager or the Oort Cloud anymore. He was more concerned with whether the aliens would allow them, and all the people of Earth, to keep on keeping on. *Explorer Two* and

Earth were nothing but sitting ducks at the moment. No, the aliens hadn't been overly hostile. Yet. But only God knew what they could do. And at any moment.

He activated his implant. "Pearls, it's Darko. Any change in the status of our new friends?"

"None at all," Adrienne replied.

"Roger. Thanks." He snapped off the circuit. "Yet" kept flashing through his mind. His nose twitched at the stench of burnt wiring. *It must be drifting throughout the ship.* He used his wristwatch to tell the main computer to run self-checks of all subordinate computers and server stacks. He hoped the short causing the stink wasn't anywhere near *Explorer Two's* "brains." Having her legs broken was bad enough.

That reminded him, he would need to transmit another report to Mission Control in—he glanced at his wrist—thirty-three minutes.

Bouchard made his way to one of the four elevators that would bypass the inner ring and take him directly to the hub. Once the doors closed, the trip took all of fourteen seconds to take him to his destination. He passed the time by using his watch to initiate a full diagnostic on the magnetron, which was the next stop on his eyes-on inspection. He exited the lift and, now weightless again in the Deck Three tunnel, fired himself toward the stern of the ship. Soon he was at the magnetron housing, which hugged the tunnel like a foam "coozie" does an ice cold can of beer.

Beer, Don thought.

A couple of years ago, he and Mags had tried their hand using the 3D printer to create something almost, but not quite, entirely unlike beer here on the ship. They won't be making *that* mistake again. Mag-Lev talked about doing it the old-fashioned way, actually brewing it from scratch after printing out hops and barley and other needed supplies. Don suggested they wait and try such an endeavor after they had completed their Voyager refit mission, when they were bored beyond belief, and the world—and their bosses back on Earth—weren't watching so closely.

Bouchard tapped on a screen to pull up the control panel of the ever-humming, giant machine that protected them at all times from so many external dangers, the hair on his arms and the back of his neck stood on end in the powerful field it generated. It tickled his insides. He readily admitted he kind of enjoyed it.

As he waited for the full diagnostic to complete, he tried to imagine the faces in the Mission Control Center at the Space X Florida campus when they get his message sixteen hours from now, the time it normally took to get a radio signal between *Explorer Two* and Earth at this distance. Some poor sap will be sitting at his comms station trying to stay awake when the transmission comes in, and it will probably take a full minute to register exactly what was said. There will be repeated playings to ensure he heard correctly: "Not of natural origin." He would call a co-worker over to see what he or she thought. Then a supervisor. Then finally Flight Control would be notified. Then people would start talking into their tele-implants. Darmstadt would be called to verify at the European Space Operations Centre. Then Korolyov. Then Beijing. Finally Washington D.C. He chuckled. "And then the arguments would start."

Don mused that NASA et al might figure out some guidance to pass along in six to twelve hours. But then he'd have to wait another sixteen hours before he could receive a response. So it would be well into tomorrow before he obtained any guidance from Earth. "Thirty-three hours, minimum," Don muttered. *Hell, we could all be dead in another thirty-three minutes!*

He tried not to think of such things and busied himself with his work. After the magnetron returned a plethora of green bubbles and bars, he moved on down the long tunnel. Next stop: the storage bins, which carried all manner of supplies and materials for their mission, and the crew's comfort and survival.

Near the bins was located two printing platforms for 3D printer #2, the one that worked fine only yesterday, and tried to print a tube of silicone sealant. A third platform was located outside the ship, to print extremely large items; this they will need to create repair parts for their broken vessel. Printer #1 was located in the maintenance bay, and wasn't working perfectly at the moment. It would need to be fixed by the time they reached Voyager. In two years. Mags figured had plenty of time to fix it, but he hadn't exactly counted on an alien attack.

A minute later, Don's order appeared on the smallest of the two interior platforms as if by magic, and he scooped it up and stuffed it in a zippered pocket. "Well, that's a relief." *Larry just received a stay of execution,* he thought. The fact that so many things were still working despite the ship nearly being torn apart was testament to the multi-national, multi-organizational craftsmanship of their wayward home.

Don spoke into his implant again. "Mags, it's Darko. I just printed out a tube of sealant for the crack in the command cabin's window."

"Oh, good," Larry replied, "that's one less thing weighing on my mind."

"You and Treads making any progress out there?"

"There's a crack in an AlON5 window!?" exclaimed Treads.

Crap. "Nothing to worry about, sweetheart. It's more of a scratch, really."

"When are you gonna realize you're a terrible liar, Donnie?"

He fell silent.

Luckily, Liev came to his rescue. "Boss, we're more-less finished out here with our inspection, if you want to hear it."

Excited to be out of his wife's line of fire, if only temporarily, Don excitedly answered. "Go ahead, Mags."

"Well, it's just as the computer reported. The accelerator tubes are all twisted up. We're going to have to recycle and re-fabricate all four. Gonna take several months."

"I figured as much," said Bouchard.

"The printers can only work so fast, you know," continued Mag-Lev. "It's funny to me; it was almost like a surgical strike. Seems like these E.T.s knew exactly where to hit us if they didn't want us to go any further, but still allow us to breathe and eat and limp... well, somewhere."

"Home," said Bouchard. "I think that was their plan, to send us packing. I guess they don't yet realize we'll need to expend every ounce of our fuel to completely stop. Forget about making it all the way back to Earth with what xenon we got!"

Mag-Lev laughed. "Hey, they're doing it for us, it seems!"

"That they are." Don checked his watch. The ship had slowed to 100,000 KPH and was holding steady.

"At least we still have thrusters," added Brea. "We can still spin this old girl around in the right direction if we have to. That's something."

Don nodded to himself. "I guess I'll take every little bit I can. Alright, let's get started. Maybe if they see you out there working, they'll lend a hand?"

"Here's to hoping. Mags out."

A new voice broke over the channel. "Commander, you might want to get back up to the command cabin."

"X-Ray..?"

"Pronto."

SIX

Bouchard launched himself through the hatch of the command cabin. He focused on the windows before him, but saw nothing that wasn't there earlier. There was the lumpy, spiky, alien ship, barely illuminated as before. He plowed into the back of his co-pilot/command chair with outstretched hands, then turned to look at Adrienne, who was staring off into space, literally. He turned his gaze back to the window and scanned the sky. After a few seconds, he looked back at Scalia.

Jack returned his glare as if to say, *"Don't you see it?"*

"What?" he finally asked.

"That!" Pearls pointed slightly off to the left.

Don looked again, but saw only the familiar star field. He squinted. Was one of them moving? He couldn't— *Wait. There!* A dark shape was moving just beyond the larger vessel. "I take it that's another ship?"

"Your guess is as good as mine," Adrienne said.

"Have any more transmissions come through, Scales?"

Scalia shook his head. "You would have heard them, I think."

Bouchard shoved himself into his seat and buckled in once more. "X-Ray, what can you tell me?"

"Not much, Commander," Isley said over the intercom. "Except that the new arrival is significantly smaller than the first ship. And it barely has a heat signature at all."

A sound burst from the loudspeakers. Bouchard listened. It was faint, and it sounded like a human voice. A female voice. A bit gurgly and... strange. But the strangest thing wasn't the characteristics of the voice.

"Is that *English?*" asked Don. "That's not them, is it? Brea, M&M, was that either of you?"

"Did that accent sound *British?*" Treads replied over a different speaker.

"Wasn't me!" This from Melodi.

Bouchard thought for a moment. "X-Ray, that's not an echo of our own transmission is it?"

"No, Commander. I've pin-pointed the source. It's definitely coming from the new arrival."

"Maybe they're broadcasting one of our old reports to Mission Control back at us?" suggested Scalia. "One that Adrienne recorded?"

Adrienne scowled and glanced over her shoulder. "Do you really think I sound like that?"

The voice returned over the loudspeakers, more clearly now. "Alright, alright!" It grew in volume, as if the speaker was now closer to the microphone. "I got it from here. Still just the seven, yes, ♓7ylÎx? You haven't picked up any others? No new spacecraft or anything?"

Chirping.

"Okay. Are we on their frequency?"

A strange set of sounds spurted from the speaker. It sounded to Don like crickets chirping and clicking underwater.

"Oh what's the big deal, Constable? What are they going to do?"

A growl this time.

X-Ray spoke softly over the internal speaker system. "That growling is coming from the larger vessel, Commander."

"Oh, please!" said the woman. "Surely you scanned their craft. Tell me they have the capability to—"

More growling.

"It's absolutely the point!"

A gurgle.

"Yes, yes, I get it, Constable. But that's their only crime. Just turn those antimatter rails off, would you? I can see from here you've got at least eight weapons trained on them, which is seven, if not eight, more than necessary. Believe me, you and your men have nothing to worry about. As you can see, that's not a battlecruiser or anything of the sort! You've intercepted too many of their movies! That's all fiction, trust me on this. Just let me handle this incident as the treaty calls for, yes?"

A click.

"Thank you."

There was one last chirp, then a strange glopping sound boomed in Don's ears. If he didn't know better, he would have thought an octopus was clearing its throat.

"Attention, explorers from Sol," the woman said, louder now. "Please turn around and head back into your designated quarantined area. If you go now, the Constable will grant you amnesty for your encroachment. If you stay, I can't promise he will not destroy your pretty, white, slender, and *very fragile* vessel. Do you understand?"

Don wondered if her stress on "very" and "fragile" was less for his crew and more for the one she called The Constable. He scrunched up his face and remained silent. This wasn't how "First Contact" occurred in any training scenario he remembered.

"Hello?" came the voice again. "Am I broadcasting? Check again, ♓7y."

Now it was Bouchard's turn to clear his throat. "Yes, hello, we're here. This is Commander Donald Bouchard. I am in command of the spaceship *Explorer Two*. I am pleased to meet you. Please understand we are merely explorers from the planet Earth. We have no weapons. Our mission is of a peaceful, scientific nature."

"Yes, even my small-minded military pals over on the big ugly ship can tell *that*," replied the woman, "which is why you're still alive."

"Great." *I think.* "So you know we don't mean anyone any harm. We are merely on a mission to find and explore the edge of our solar system."

"Well, you found it. Congratulations. Now go home."

Bouchard glanced at Adrienne, who looked like a deer staring into headlights, and couldn't help but chuckle. "Ma'am? I must admit I am at a loss. We just made what is possibly the most incredible discovery in all of human history! We can't simply turn and leave now that we—"

"What was that?"

"Um, I said we can't leave now that—"

"No, the other part."

Don blinked. "Excuse me?"

"What is your discovery? The biggest one in 'all of human history'?"

"Well, ma'am, I think it's obvious. My crew and I just discovered intelligent life actually exists beyond the confines of our world. We want to get to know you, to share knowledge, become friends, if possible..?"

"Look, Commander, I know you're a little behind in the current events department here, so I'll try to make this simple for you. The Constable, who is in charge of this sector, know your people well. Not as well as I do, of course, I have been assigned to study Earth in depth, but he knows humans well enough. Luckily for you and your crew, more level minds prevailed today, and I was notified in time... *this time.*"

Another growl. Don guessed it once again came from the larger ship.

"Now, please," the woman continued, "I'm sure there are a thousand questions banging around in your meaty brain housings, but believe me when I tell you, there's no time for a big philosophical discussion about how and why you are only aware of the last forty or fifty ▷♑coys of Earth's history. For your own health, and for the sake of everyone on Earth, turn your little tin can around, and don't come this way again."

Bouchard and the others exchanged glances. "But ma'am! I don't...we don't—"

"No buts," she said. "Now listen closely, this is important. When you get back to Earth, tell your world leaders that the ⦸♈*)(*♈⦸ Council is kindly restating, for the record, its mandate regarding the Sol quarantine, and not taking adverse action at this time for the blatant violation of the treaty. They will all know what you are talking about. In case they deny it, which they probably will, and refuse to share it with even other sections of their own government—like I said I know your kind well—I will read it to you. No. I will summarize, since we've only got another few more ♍i1s before the General loses *all* his patience and mans his guns and pulls the trigger himself."

Don tried to speak, but his jaw merely hung slack.

"If you are not recording this conversation already," continued the woman, "I suggest you begin now. I will give you five seconds with which to do so."

A harsh glop resounded through the cabin as a grasshopper-hippo coughed.

"Constable please, this will only take a ♍i1 or two. Ready? 'Earthlings' —it technically translates to 'Earthers,' but that sounds strange even to me—'it is understandable you want to explore your environment. You may do so all you wish, but you must remain within the confines of your solar system, which is defined as, 'a radius of no more than one hundred twenty of your Astronomical

Units from your star in any given direction', rather than merely stating 'the limit of your star's magnetosphere or heliosphere'. This way you may not take advantage of the irregular, teardrop shape of these regions. Due to past transgressions, ignoring or outright disregarding this mandate and entering interstellar space will put your planet at risk of invasion, up to and including societal annihilation by the Allied Federated Systems of ⦸♈*)(*♈⦸.' That is it in a nutshell. What do you say... Ka-peesh?" Then, in a softer voice, "What? Well no, of course these humans won't understand, but the message will get to the right people on Earth eventually."

After that speech, Bouchard was so far from understanding that all he wanted to do was to curl up into a ball, stick his thumb in his mouth, and wait for his mommy to fly out past Neptune to come get him. Unfortunately, that wasn't an option at the moment. "Ma'am, I don't even know where to begin with regard to questions, but I can tell you that we have a bit of a problem on our hands when it comes to heading back to Earth."

"What's your problem?" she asked.

"Well, for starters, our engines are torn up, thanks to your friends in the big ship there."

"What?" The woman pulled away from her microphone and continued in a harsh tone. "You stupid ⅁℮⇕! Why would you damage their engines if you want them to change course and head home?"

A deep gurgling and some clicking followed.

"Yes, it's *very* fragile! Had you bothered to run a quick scan before opening fire you would have discovered that!"

More chirping.

"Well I doubt it, or they wouldn't be about to commit suicide crossing the Heliopause, now would they?"

Well that doesn't sound promising, thought Bouchard. *Would we not have made it?*

"I can't believe you fired on such a vessel!"

Click, click, glurp.

"There are other ways to slow them down! This is why you were instructed to call me first before doing anything!"

Gurgling and chirping.

"Nowadays, yes! These humans of this era are not like the others."

A chirp.

"Orders be damned. Look what's happened now. You've got a quarter of the fleet paralleling us, the Princess herself watching, and her mother threatening to clear her schedule for the entire ♑♏ just in case this situation gets out of hand. If it does, she'll have to answer to all Eleven Queendoms as to why her Navy couldn't properly contain the Scourge of Sector 189. *Again!*"

Don looked at Pearls.

Pearls look at Don.

Something resembling a scoff came over the speaker. "Can we send a repair drone over?"

Chirping. Squealing. Then what sounded like banging and smashing of equipment, then more squealing.

"Oh Constable, for ⭯ℯɤ↕'s sake!"

Don heard chirping again, then more sounds from what seemed like a different individual.

"They're doing what?" asked the woman, in a soft voice. Then louder, "Constable. No. Wait. Listen to me—"

Fluttering. Squealing. Buzzing.

"Damn your orders!" screamed the woman. "These are peaceful explorers, not soldiers!"

Don swore he heard cooing.

"For once, Constable, do the right thing. Just once. For me."

Squelching, gurgling, fervent clicking.

"Are you serious?"

Silence.

"Well, I should have known. Remember this, Constable. There will be repercussions!" the woman screamed. "But you will wait to carry out your orders until I follow my ministry's policy and have performed my scan!"

Two clicks.

"You have your job, Constable, I have mine."

Shuffling followed. Then a final, distant squeal.

"That man is impossible. Cockroaches," she muttered. The woman then addressed the *Explorer Two* one last time. "Earth ship. I would suggest you sit down and make yourself comfortable for the next thirty seconds. Our ♐B& scan is somewhat intrusive. It will have a much higher chance of success if you move as little as possible, no matter how uncomfortable you feel. Minor movements are fine, just no walking or jumping about. Do you understand? Commander Bouchard? This is very important."

"Um..."

"We must do this before we can commit to any kind of repairs," she added.

"Uh, yes," he replied, "understood. We'll settle in."

"Good. Ensure your crew understands."

Bouchard looked around the command cabin, then clicked on the intercom. "Did everyone catch that? Treads, Mags? X-Ray, M&M?"

"Got it, pet," called his wife. "Mag-Lev and I have already activated our magnetic boots and are just hanging out on top of what's left of accelerator number three."

"Good. Everyone else?"

"M&M, wilco!" said Melodi. "I needed a break anyway."

"Roger, Mel."

"This is X-Ray. Holding position."

"Roger, Ray." Don looked behind him. Scalia was giving him the thumbs up. "Okay." Lastly, he turned to Pearls. Her eyes were closed and she seemed to be praying. "Adrienne? Are we five-by-five?"

A couple of seconds later, she turned her head his way and opened her large, brown eyes. They were wet.

"Hey, listen. All you have to do is just sit back and relax. This sounds like merely one of their procedures. Then I think they'll fix us up and we'll be on our way."

She took a deep breath. "Then why is my gut telling me to flee?" she whispered.

Don stared at her, but said nothing. He had learned long ago to trust feminine intuition. A foreboding fell upon him, but as Commander, he had to remain strong for the crew. He suppressed his new found fear and called out. "Ma'am, we're ready!" Then in a softer voice, "I don't know exactly what our friend has in store, but—"

The next instant, the cabin glowed purple. Don saw a wide beam slice through the ceiling, stretching from the left wall to the right, but not cutting or being destructive in any way. It seemed like intense radiation, the violet light somehow going *through* solid objects. It "washed" downward with not even the slightest sound. It was the brightest light Don had ever seen, brighter than the noon-day sun in the Arizona sky. And it was much hotter than that Arizona sun, too. Was his skin starting to burn?

Pearls yelped. "Ow! My necklace! It's burning my skin!"

"Try not to move, Adrienne!" Don called to her. "The woman said not to move!"

"But it hurts... so bad..." she muttered.

"Just hold on another few seconds, Adrienne!" Bouchard gritted his teeth and felt his insides cooking. He heard a groan from behind him. Scalia was in pain as well.

Pearls screamed. "My legs! They're on fire!"

Her words were an instant reminder of the accident. After her experimental supersonic plane had crashed in the high desert of Nevada, U.S. Air

Force doctors had done a superb job of repairing her mangled lower half. Since the age of twenty-one, Adrienne had sported synthetic legs. Even in a bathing suit, it was nearly impossible to tell where the flesh stopped and the synthetic flesh began. Don was almost jealous of the abilities she gained; it was impossible to keep up with her in a foot race. Why, she could reach speeds of—

SEVEN

Don Bouchard stirred, as if from a long sleep. But had he been asleep? Sounds entered his mind, but none sounded familiar. Sparks flashed in the darkness, but he could focus on none of them. He tried to open his eyes, but wasn't sure he had succeeded. The world around him was dark, but not totally black. He opened his mouth to take a breath, as if for the first time. What was that taste? He'd never tasted that before. A smell entered his nostrils. *What the hell is that?* Everything seemed... odd. Not necessarily foreign. Just different.

He tried to move.

"Relax," said a female voice. It wasn't familiar. Or was it?

He then heard gurgling noises. Clicking. He had definitely heard those noises before. Only they sounded a bit different, too.

"Try not to move," a woman said, "your body isn't ready."

He recognized the voice now. It simply wasn't amplified electronically. Don's mouth moved, but only groans came out.

"Shhh. You are safe now. As long as I stay smarter than the Royal Military, you and your crew will be safe. Which shouldn't be too terribly hard."

Bouchard tried to relax. He opened his eyes again, and saw a bright light now. Everything was blurry. "My... My eyes..." He gurgled the words in the back of his throat.

"Close them. They are not ready just yet."

A thought struck him. "My crew!" He coughed and sputtered fluid into his mouth.

"Please! You may rupture the delicate tissue before it's cured! It's only been two Earth days. I need to let the process continue for just one more. I will check on you again soon. Sleep, my friend."

A bright blue light flooded his vision, and Don Bouchard lost consciousness.

EIGHT

Don and Pearls meandered down a dark hallway that looked more like it had been tunneled out of granite than built in an alien spacedock. Nooks and crannies of all shapes and sizes glowed from a light source he couldn't see. Or possibly not understand.

"I don't get it, are we prisoners?" Adrienne asked. The whites of her large eyes gleamed brightly, in stark contrast with her dark skin, which nearly blended with the walls in the dim light. "Will we be able to continue our mission? Will we even be allowed to return to the *Explorer?*"

Don halted and stared straight ahead. "All very good questions."

Adrienne stopped too, and crossed her arms. "I just wish we could see the others. They're in one of these caves," Pearls said, eyeballing one of the many round, sealed doors around her, "I just don't know which."

"They'd better be," Don spat.

"Snine-yl-curix—or whatever her name is—said they were here. You don't trust her? She did save us from getting blown out of the sky."

"I'll feel a lot better when I see them for myself."

She breathed deeply. "I hope Larry is okay. I know how he gets when he's apart from me for too long. I just want to let him know I'm here, that I'm alive and safe. He worries so."

Don dropped his arms and spun on his heel. "That's it. I'm getting answers. *Now.*" He stomped down the tunnel, towards one of the only rooms to which he had access: the bridge of the small, alien science vessel.

"Wait. Darko, wait! I don't think this is the best way to—"

He tuned her out, his thoughts falling upon Brea, fearing she may also be wondering where he was. And if he was still alive.

The dimly lit tunnels of the small alien ship were novel for the first twenty-four hours after he and Pearls were able to stand on their own two feet, but now Bouchard had seen all there was to see. Or rather, everything the aliens would allow him to see, which wasn't much. He and Adrienne were told they could wander the ship alone, but they were warned not to touch anything except the food and drink dispensers, and the toilets—if they could be called that.

The "woman" who had spoken English to them over the loudspeakers of *Explorer Two* called herself "❧9ylÎx." She had to type it on a display for Don to comprehend the name, and he murdered the pronunciation every time he tried to say it. But her name wasn't important. The fact she promised answers, however, was. *It is past time for those answers, and I'm not going to let her blow me off again!* Don's resolve surprised even him.

"Donnie, please, let's just wait a little longer," Pearls whispered as she rushed to catch up.

The tunnel before them opened automatically at their approach, more like the mouth of a living beast than merely a door, and Bouchard burst onto the alien bridge, piping mad, and not for the first time. The corners were black, but the ceiling glowed from stem to stern with holographic displays. He saw Earth in one of those displays, serene and peaceful. He hoped that was a current view, and not a recording of some kind.

In the center stood a large, round, brightly illuminated console. ୨9ylÎx sat on one side of it, her many appendages dancing slowly and deliberately over glowing bulbs and shiny tendrils. Her shipmate, another insect-like creature who she called "♓7ylÎx", sat next to her. Don had rarely seen them apart. The two were basically the same; their wings had the same multi-hued iridescence, their thoraxes were the same size, their tracheae and mal... malphi...something—whatever those front tubules were called, Don couldn't remember—appeared identical. He could only tell them apart because one could speak English, and the other could not.

Three other seats grew out of the granite-colored flooring on the other side of the console, which Bouchard assumed was the command station for the entire vessel. There were no other 'stations' in the room, and no windows to be found anywhere.

"Hello, Commander!" ୨9ylÎx said in a peppy voice, sounding genuinely happy to see him. But then, she sounded like that every time she saw him. "Did you enjoy your dinner?"

Adrienne plopped down on what may or may not have been a bench that circumnavigated the roughly roundish room, and put her head in her hands.

Don knew what she was thinking. She was certain he was going to screw things up with his impatience. *We'll see.* He pointed to one of the many massive holographic screens above him. "☙9ylÎx, if I'm reading that right—and frankly I don't know how I am reading it at all—the last ship left the area hours ago, and is now several light years away at this point. May we finally get some answers?"

☙9ylÎx looked up with three of her eight black eyes. One of these found Pearls, and locked on her lithe form. "You sound angry, Commander."

"Well... that's because I am!"

B7yl^x raised one antenna and clicked twice.

"Yes, you're right, he has been very patient," ☙9ylÎx agreed. She made what sounded like a sigh, then spun her chair around and faced Bouchard, all eyes trained upon him. "Commander, you are correct, all the ships have gone, and it is safe to speak freely now. Again, I want to apologize for being so rude when I first contacted you. I had to take a hard stance in front of the military, or they would have brushed me aside and destroyed you in the blink of an eye. And I am sorry I've had to keep you 'in the dark' as you say, these last twenty-five hours. It was merely a precaution. With that said, what are your questions?"

Don calmed down almost instantly. "Thank you." He turned to Adrienne and smiled.

Pearls looked up. The expression on her face said, "That actually worked?"

"Okay," Bouchard said. "First, while you've reassured me again and again that my crew is fine and in fact here on this ship somewhere, I haven't seen hide nor hair of them. You told me it's been three days since the 'incident', since what I call First Contact. Three days! I want to see them, especially my wife. Second, tell me, just how did we get here? Do you have some sort of teleportation technology? Because I don't remember ever leaving our ship. Three, how is it that you can speak English as well as we can, and no other alien we've met or talked to can? Who are you, exactly? *What* are you?"

Clicking and gurgling noises came from ♓7ylÎx.

♋9ylÎx turned two eyes to her companion. "You're probably right. I hope their hearts can handle the stress of the revelation."

Clicking.

Don swallowed. Hard.

The gray insectoid leaned toward him. "Commander, I'm sorry to inform you that *Time* has erased your history. The natural oscillations of your star that causes periodic ice ages and global warming—on all planets, not just yours—plus eon after eon of devastating wars that you've waged against yourselves and other alien species, has taken its toll." Three eyes turned towards ♓7ylÎx.

"It's a wonder any humans have survived at all. I've been monitoring their planet for how long?"

Two clicks and a blop.

"That's right, over sixty ▷♑coys now. As far as they know, their civilization is the first to invent electricity! They think they're the first humans to ever venture into space!"

The alien spoke as if Don and Pearls weren't there, but he felt as though her words were strictly for their sake.

The other shook her head.

A brief silence followed. Adrienne must have either missed the cue that they were being lectured, or didn't care. "Ma'am? What is a 'coy'-whatever?" she asked.

"A ▷♑coy?" ☙9ylÎx corrected. "That is almost exactly two hundred and eleven of your Earth years."

Don's eyes fluttered. "And you've been studying our world for... how many of those?"

"Coming up on sixty-two."

"So... you're saying, you've been watching us for *twelve thousand years?*"

"In Earth years, yes." The woman replied. "Actually, it's closer to thirteen thousand."

Adrienne's jaw was slack when Don turned to see if she had heard the same thing he heard. "How long do you live, anyway?" she exclaimed.

"If we're lucky, a hundred or so ▷♑coys. The record is a hundred and forty-seven, since we started keeping accurate records."

"Wait," Bouchard said, "you people live twenty to thirty thousand years?"

"Not all. Some of us aren't so lucky in this life."

"But," said Adrienne, "you yourself have been studying our world since... since basically the birth of our civilization?"

"You mean the birth of the *current* civilization on Earth, yes," ᔕ9ylîx corrected. "That's when my official study began. I was assigned ♏42☼—or the Sol system as you call it—when it was clear your planet was coming out of another Ice Age. The previous custodian of ♏42☼3⦸♈=⊗ had planned to return to study you. That was prior to your planet acquiring the =× identifier, indicating that it was off-limits to all but authorized personnel." She performed what sounded like "tsk-tsk-tsk." "Like I said, some of us aren't so lucky in this life."

♓7ylîx fluttered, creaked, chirped and clicked.

"Agreed." Eight eyes darted back and forth between Don and Pearls. "You Earthlings always end up being Enemy Number One! Why is that? Why does your kind always have to fear and destroy what you don't understand? ☪3uiîp, the former custodian of Earth, was an ancient, wise, peaceful soul. Not to mention our friend. We mourned her for a full ♍i1▷♑coy."

"Humans killed her?"

"In what you would call 'cold blood', at their first meeting. We have a different saying, by the way, as none of us are endothermic. I'm sure at least one of you already surmised this."

Don swallowed again. *I hope they're not going to hold us responsible for something our ancestors did millennia ago!*

"Our Council deliberated for a long time," ঌ9ylÎx continued. "Too long for most. The order finally came. Our Border Patrol, augmented by the Royal Guard, wiped out your Armada. And your colonies, too, the ones that had fared so well, even though Earth was an icy wasteland for so many thousands of years and couldn't support them. They were successful, but they were parasites on hundreds of worlds in the galaxy. I felt nothing. Not sadness. Not joy. Not regret. Only that justice was served."

"You committed genocide?" Pearls screamed.

"That would be of the highest immorality!" the woman said. "Of course we didn't commit genocide. You are living proof of that!"

"A holocaust, then."

ঌ9ylÎx seemed to consider the word.

Her companion chirped a few times.

"Ah yes, I remember now," said ঌ9ylÎx, "the near genocide of their second world war. I suppose you could say this was similar. But for a much different reason. We did what we did for the safety, and frankly, the continuing existence, of the population of the galaxy. Humans are violent. Destructive. Greedy. Unreasonable. Unconscionable."

"Their armada," Don said. "Those ships weren't ours. Those people weren't us."

"They were just like you."

"Not like me. Not like her," he said, motioning to Pearls, who sat on her hands and stared straight ahead at nothing. "Not like any of my crew."

The aliens turned and looked at one another. ঌ9ylÎx nodded. "No. Not like you," she agreed. "You and your crew, Commander, are the first human explorers any of us have ever met who appear reasonable. You're also the first to venture out here in a fragile, unarmed tin can instead of a warship ready to eliminate anything and everything it happens to find."

Don chewed his lip, and looked back at Adrienne. He wondered if she was thinking what he was. That the aliens obviously hadn't found their nuclear missiles.

Not yet, anyway.

"It's fortunate for all involved, really," ঌ9ylÎx went on, "that most of your population now tends to remain on Earth or on the moons of the outer planets, and not venture into the great expanse. It's understandable, especially since Edene^a was reduced to a desert wasteland—you now call it 'Mars'—there isn't another lush, green, watery world for dozens of light years in any direction. Each time this is discovered, word reaches the ears of everyone on your planet, and lucky for the rest of the galaxy, most humans stay put. Lucky for the rest of us, you fleshy types don't fare too well on any of the other systems nearby—even with proper technology. And then, as happens every now and again, Earth's ice ages wipe the slate clean, or nearly so. They finally bring a pause to the human need to expand and conquer. If not an end. But it is close enough."

Bouchard noticed Pearls had began to rock back and forth, her brow low, her eyes glossed over. "Did you destroy Mars?"

ঌ9ylÎx's eyes all seemed to widen at once. "My kind would never decimate an entire planet's ecosystem, even to rid the universe of a scourge like Humanity! We may wipe out the parasite itself, but never all the life on its surface. No, Mars was like that many, many ▷♑coys ago. Not even the oldest in our society remembers a green Mars. But our history reports it was once a paradise. What you call 'Mother Nature' brought an end to that world on its own."

"I see," said Don. "I had to ask."

"Here is something you'll find interesting, Commander. Before the armistice of 6542 K.S.E.—that's your own King Solomon's Era, a little over ten thousand Earth years ago—humans used to live two to five ▷♑coys. Noah, the most famous of your Generals, lived nearly five, if I remember correctly."

Five coy-things? Don thought. *A thousand years!?* "Are you telling me it's true? The ancient texts? The Holy Bible says Noah lived about 950 years, if I remember correctly. But I always assumed those 'years' were actually 'new moons', and an interpretation just got mixed up at some point. For instance, you get a normal human lifespan of 73 years if you divide 950 by thirteen, thirteen being the number of new moons in any given year. That made sense to me. But there's nothing in the Bible about him being a General. Not that I remember, anyway." He looked at Adrienne.

She shrugged. "I only know the Mahabharata. And I've not exactly memorized it."

One of ♋9ylÎx's eyes twisted to look toward her companion, who was busy working on the bulbous controls in front of her with delicate, insectoid limbs. "See? Just as I said. Clueless."

♓7ylÎx cooed.

"I agree. It's not their fault."

Don thought of ♓7ylÎx as female also, simply due to the creature's mannerisms, but he wasn't certain. He admitted to himself he was assigning human characteristics to beings he had never even known existed before yesterday, and that male and female characteristics probably weren't universal. Or were they?

"Okay," Adrienne said, suddenly snapping out of her trance and standing up. "The Mahabharata records a global flood occurring at the time of a man named Mana, and that he and his family were the only ones to survive after taking seeds and animals with him to repopulate the Earth."

"Like Noah?" asked Don.

"Yes," she replied. "Surprise, your holy book says a lot of same things mine does. And probably a great many others as well."

♋9ylÎx seemed to chuckle. "She's right about that."

Don sighed. "Brea always believed all those stories were analogies. Parables. Warnings. Stories written down to try to explain things no one could explain, or to control a population, or to scare us into being good people."

Pearls' hands were on her hips now. "So are the stories true? Did any of them actually happen?"

♋9ylÎx laughed. "We will be here for great many ♍i1▷♑coys if we start from the beginning and I tell you what I know! We may have time someday.

But for now, regarding the deluges of Earth... I witnessed many, many people building boats. They took on board anything and everything they could, including animals and plants. The flood that happened on my watch wasn't exactly global, but it was widespread and devastating. It killed most humans, animals and insects that didn't live in the mountainous regions. But it was nothing truly special; these deluges always happen at the end of ice ages, when the glaciers begin to melt. There have been many of your 'global floods' over the eons. I don't know which flood in particular your ancient texts speak of—it could have been the one that occurred about eleven thousand Earth years ago—but many survivors likely experienced one of these great floods and lived through it, and passed the story on to their children."

"Many... floods..." whispered Don.

"Yes," replied ৡ9ylÎx. "Floods, meteor and cometary impacts, the list goes on. Life, especially human life, survives natural disasters due to its resourcefulness. Over and over again. Commander, it was not a natural disaster that nearly destroyed you. It was yourselves. Your violent nature. The Earthlings waged war on the various races of this great galaxy many times. The ⦸♈*)(*♈⦸ Council nearly ordered your complete extinction—yes, genocide—not merely the destruction of your military might. But the populace of the galaxy spoke out against it, and leaders of all the countries and kingdoms of Earth pleaded for mercy. The Council offered the human race a deal. The humans didn't like it, but in the end your leaders agreed that it was better than the alternative."

"What was the deal?" asked Adrienne.

"The deal was to drastically shorten the human life span. It was believed that if the troublesome humans didn't live so long, they would not have time to grow so jaded, so... heartless. Not enough time to stay focused and build armadas that could reach the stars. Never reach other civilizations they could dominate, enslave, and steal their lands. No time to do much beyond worry about their own meager existence on their own tiny world. And it has proven to work, for over ten thousand Earth years. It was a good choice for all involved, even the humans." ♌9ylÎx's mandibles curled, resembling a smile. "For even existing only half a ▷♑coy is better than not ever existing at all."

More chirping and gurgling.

"Commander Bouchard. ♓7y wants to know something, and so do I. Why did you come out here? What made you come?"

"Nothing *made* us. We just wanted to know what's out here. I guess humans are curious by nature. Another of our less-than-desirable traits, I imagine."

"Curiosity isn't undesirable. Don't ever think such a thing. We admire your curiosity, and your bravery to do what it takes to discover new things. Speaking of which, this was a one-way trip, wasn't it? You never intended on going home, did you?"

Bouchard paused before answering. "No. We couldn't have turned around if you had demanded it. Our ship wasn't built to do so."

ঌ9ylÎx nodded. "So what was your mission?"

"To put it simply, to reach interstellar space and report our findings back to Earth."

"And that's it? You weren't looking for a wayward space probe by any chance, were you?"

"Well, that was a secondary mission. That's why we chose this particular route out of the solar system. We haven't heard from it in about a hundred and fifty years. We had hoped to repair it and release it back on its original trajectory."

Don could have sworn ঌ9ylÎx smiled. "In that case," she said, standing from her chair and balancing graciously on four thin legs, "I have something to show you."

♓7ylÎx chirped.

"Yes, yes, don't worry."

"What did she say?" asked Pearls.

All of ঌ9ylÎx eyes darted in Adrienne's direction. "*She?*" She smiled. "You're very perceptive for a human."

Bouchard turned to Perle and muttered, "I knew that."

NINE

Don stared at the lone object in the center of the large hangar. "You're kidding me."

৯9ylÎx chirped and cooed. It sounded like pure delight. Standing before them, in all its space-weathered glory, was Voyager 2, illuminated by bright spotlights from somewhere in the depths of the darkness above them.

"How long have you had it?" asked Pearls.

"I've had the pattern stored for about one of your centuries, half a ▷♑coy," said ৯9ylÎx. "I was with the Border Patrol when they intercepted Voyager 1 in 2012 of your Common Era, right after it crossed the heliopause. Its fate was debated in the Council for several weeks. I argued that if it was destroyed while still transmitting information to Earth, the humans may send an envoy after it to learn what became of it, and hasten another interstellar incident. I knew of your weapons and spacecraft capabilities back in that era better than anyone, and witnessed before the Council that neither you nor the tiny probe were any kind of threat to even a pupas' toy mUu❖i, let alone the Federated Worlds. But the treaty was the treaty, the all-coveted Earth-⦸♈*⌘↑m Pact. It was steadfast in its mandate, and Earth had violated it. Like the two Pioneer spacecraft that came before, the Voyager 1 had to be destroyed as well. And what was right on its heels? A second one! Almost instantly, the same fate was decided for Voyager 2."

"But," Don interrupted, "NASA briefed us extensively on Voyager 2. They have, on-record, data analyzed by a company in Lawrence, Kansas that dates back to 2027, when it finally went dark."

"You have me to thank for that," beamed ♋9ylÎx with pride. "I was able to talk the Council into waiting until 2030 of Earth's Common Era before the order was sent to the Border Patrol to destroy the quaint little craft. Both of them. I told them that waiting just another one-quarter ♍i1▷♑coy would give the power cells time to completely die—the Earthlings were expecting this, after all—and so the people of Earth would not become suspicious and try to determine why their probe went silent so abruptly. Uninhabited stealth drones shadowed it twenty-five hours a day from 2019 to 2030 by your calendar, just to ease the minds of the masses following it in the news, not to mention the small mind of the Constable. Luckily, I am smarter than him."

♓7ylÎx chirped loudly.

♋9ylÎx chuckled. "Yes! My smallest claw is smarter than that drone! I was able to trick the Constable into allowing me to perform a facsimile scan just prior to the incineration date. The machine standing before you is a perfect replica from the year 2029, down to the microscopic flaws in the grooves of Mr. Carl Sagan's gold record! And with non-organic matter such as this, our facsimile error rate is a solid *zero* percent!" She stated this last fact with not a small hint of superiority.

"So," said Adrienne, "she wouldn't have been out there for us to catch and release even if the Constable hadn't shown up."

"No," said ঌ9ylÎx.

"I guess that explains why we hadn't picked her up on any sensor or telescope yet," said Don. "I thought perhaps we were simply too far away and Voyager was simply too small."

"There is light at the end of the tunnel, or at least I have hope that there is," continued ঌ9ylÎx. "When the ⦸♈*)(*♈⦸ Council makes its decision in your favor—and I suspect they will—I plan to release this little bird back into the sky, with a full compliment of protector drones to ensure its safety from both natural and sentient threats. I've even upgraded those terrible nuclear power cells with a ♑x(*), which you might call a type of 'zero-point energy' device, which will draw energy directly from the vacuum of space. Voyager will broadcast data back to Earth for another half-million of your years! Of course, there's not much to see out here between Sol and the solar system you call Ross 248, but with its improved equipment, it will give your scientists 'something to chew on', as I've heard say. For instance, *all* of the probe's equipment can now be switched back on with no worry at all of running out of power. Plus I replaced its plasma spectrometer and Cosmic Ray System with devices that can make measurements from 0.007 to 1.3 billion electron volts! I won't go into how big of a pain in the abdomen it was marrying our nano♌♒ technology with your antiquated circuit boards."

Bouchard shook his head. "But why? Why do all this?"

"Why? This is a beautiful piece of your history!" exclaimed ៚9ylÎx. "It, along with its sister spacecraft, expanded your understanding of the outer planets of your solar system by an immeasurable factor. It opened innumerable doors to humankind's understanding of the interstellar medium near your star. Don't you want to preserve it?"

"Well of course. I mean... I guess," he replied. "It just seems kind of pointless now, doesn't it?" Bouchard looked around. "I mean, the *Explorer Two* is so far advanced from this thing, we could almost fly circles around it. We were only going to refit the old girl just to say we did it. With our ship relaying back to Earth a thousand more measurements than Voyager ever could, and doing so every second of every day, the whole idea was more for space history and nostalgia than anything else. And now we're in a spaceship—no, a *starship*—that can likely travel faster than light itself, and is probably capable of things I could never dream of! This ancient piece of machinery here is the equivalent of a hand-written note when compared to transmitting data via quantum entanglement!"

"But even a hand-written note has value, Commander. It allows a being to encode information and transfer that message to another being without the two being present at the same time. A note, by its very nature, assumes an educated society, in which two people understand common encrypted data, which you call 'language', and with this language you can share complex ideas. It may be pointless to repair Voyager from your perspective, perhaps, but what of the people of Earth?"

"Yes," Don agreed. "What of the people of Earth? We weren't scheduled to rendezvous with this thing—well, not *this* one, the original—for another couple of years. If you wake it up early, or don't let us continue our mission, guess what's going to happen? As soon as this bird starts sending data that its original instruments were never designed to be able to collect, and lighting up the receivers back on Earth thanks to what, tenfold more wattage than ever before?"

"Twentyfold!" ঌ9ylÎx interjected.

Pearls' eyes bulged. "I know some people in Canberra who might have a heart attack..."

"Twenty times more—" Don shook his head. "As soon as all that starts to happen, don't you think the scientists back on Earth will get suspicious then? It will be *worse* than if the damn thing had abruptly went silent out of the blue after being shot out of the sky!"

His last word echoed throughout the large space, and silence filled the large, dark hangar.

"It won't matter by then," ঌ9ylÎx said.

"It won't matter? Many of our scientists work for the military," Don added. "If my ancient ancestors were as much trouble as you claim they were, it goes to reason that you people would want to keep humans as scientifically in the dark as possible, lest we build another armada in another few coy-things, and are once again ready for the Border Patrol!"

"You don't understand." ♋9ylÎx smiled, or at least Don thought she did. "Even before this most recent incident, we have been watching your society closely. For the past several ▷♑coys, ♓7y and I have submitted a formal report once every ♍i1▷♑coy. But today we received new instructions. We are to report to the Council on a continual basis, daily if necessary, focusing on any and all significant human advancements. Commander, Ms. Perle, I believe in your species, otherwise you two would not be standing before me. I believe, as does ♓7y, that humans have the capability of using science for the betterment of their kind, rather than the detriment of themselves and other species, on Earth and across the galaxy. I believe you can use what you learn to feed everyone on your planet, improve medicine, further education, all the while balancing this with security for all. Some focus in the Art of War is ironically necessary to maintain long-term peace, but pouring the greater amount of your efforts and resources into conquering endeavors is what brought about the treaty in the first place. I do not wish to see another 'deal' made to your detriment, and I especially don't wish to see your world come to harm. I wish we could return you and warn your people that we will be paying close attention. Unfortunately, we no longer can."

"Why not?" asked Adrienne.

"We have new guidance now," ♋9ylÎx replied. "You see, upgrading Voyager and releasing her will not matter, because by the time I do so, the Council will have made its decision, one way or another."

"Its decision?" Pearls asked.

"Yes. A decision I plan to be made in your favor."

Don and Adrienne eyeballed one another.

"I will explain when we are back on the bridge," said ❧9ylÎx. "Come. I must check on the progression of the reconstruction project that is occurring in Lab Three."

TEN

❧9ylîx climbed into her chair, one Don could never sit in due to the fact it was designed for the comfort of a giant insect, and stared at a colorful display. "Ah! Everything appears fine and on-schedule!" She continued tapping on the holographic "screen" embedded in the large, round console. "Perhaps a few small adjustments..."

Don leaned over to try to see if he could recognize some of the characters on the display, but from his angle he could only see a few circles. He waited for the alien to explain, but she was silent as her claws danced on the swirling colors. A few seconds later, Bouchard noticed she had turned two of her midnight eyes toward him. He gasped at the realization, and felt as though he had just been caught with his hand in the cookie jar. He drew away.

"So," said Pearls. "About this decision you spoke of..?"

❧9ylîx pointed four eyes in their direction and kept working. "I'm both pleased, and admittedly a little terrified, to announce that your presence here has hastened the ♏42☼3⦸♈=⊗ decision timeline."

Don's brow furrowed. "The what?"

Adrienne shook her head. "What does that mean?"

"It means the Council is preparing to meet in the coming ♍i1▷♑coy to determine whether to merely increase patrols, or destroy your kind altogether, once and for all. I'm sorry. We just received the communiqué a few ♍i1s ago."

"Oh." Bouchard muttered. "Great."

"If it were up to me," ♋9ylÎx continued, "I'd be willing to give your kind another chance right now. Or at least some members of your species." A claw opened toward them, and she added, "Obviously, or you wouldn't have been brought on board. But it's not up to me, it is up to the ⦸♈*)(*♈⦸ Council, who oversees the governance of all the Federated Worlds. They're the ones who commissioned the Royal Border Patrol all those ▷♑coys ago. They're the ones pointing several anti-matter weapons at Earth. They're the ones making sure humans never again wreak their destructive nature on the peaceful peoples of this beautiful galaxy."

Bouchard let out a long breath. "So if the decision is to destroy us..."

"It won't be," ♋9ylÎx assured him. "I am confident I can sway the Council's decision in your favor. But, there is a slight chance I will fail. If so, you and your crew, Commander, will be all that's left of the human race. A tiny number, but six humans is not zero humans. The race will survive. As long as I stay one step ahead of the Council and the military, that is."

Pearls gave Don a dirty look. "Negative Nancy!" She turned back to the alien. "So, if the decision goes our way, I assume the Council will make an announcement that will be heard all over Earth? And remind or inform everyone of the treaty? Then you can come clean and release fake Voyager 2 and let Earth continue to learn from it. Is this correct?"

"Yes."

"And you can let us go on with our journey?"

"Your journey? I'm not certain the Council will allow that, no matter their decision."

"What about going home?" asked Don.

"That could be a possibility. There are factors ♓7y and I must consider. Do we alert the Council of your existence at that point? Or do we keep you a secret to them and to your own people lest the Council intercepts your news broadcasts and discovers you? Could we hide you among them by changing your appearance? And let you live out your lives on your home world? Would you even want to return after all the wonders I will eventually show you? All these things we must discuss."

Bouchard fell silent.

"What exactly is a mil-coy?" asked Pearls. "I'm just curious as to how long Earth may have."

"A ♍i1▷♑coy is about half of one of your centuries." ♋9ylÎx replied.

"Fifty years!" exclaimed Bouchard. "We'll be dead by then!"

"Oh, you absolutely will not! And anyway, a decision likely won't take that long. Please know that ♓7y and I will put in a terrific word for the current generation on your behalf. You were prepared to sacrifice yourselves all in the name of acquiring knowledge rather than territory for your people! That is very honorable."

"Sacrifice ourselves?" Don pondered the idea. "Well, I guess you can say that. Eventually each of us would—will—die out here. But I had hoped not to die before detecting at least one Oort Cloud object, something none of our probes have ever been able to do in two hundred years. Voyager 2 was calculated to reach the cloud in another hundred years or so, hence why we planned to rendezvous with it and replace its power cell and wake it up for the first time in a hundred and fifty years. I mean sure, we would have beaten her to the cloud with our ion drive, so really it was more for nostalgia than anything else. We humans are sentimental like that."

"Like I said, you were going to sacrifice yourselves," ঌ9ylÎx said.

"Well not anytime soon."

"On the contrary, it would have been much sooner than you likely believe. As I'm sure you're aware, the *Explorer Two* could not have protected you from the interstellar radiation that would have flooded the ship as soon as you fully crossed the heliopause of your sun."

Don noticed Adrienne staring at him, her brows together. "Actually," he said, "we were counting on *Explorer Two's* H_3O-filled exterior walls and its magnetic field to protect us from the background cosmic radiation we knew we'd encounter. It has done a good job up to this point, our detectors still read radiation levels far below—"

"Oh, Commander!" The gray insectoid chuckled. "There is a reason our ships' hulls are engineered with the ☼⩞❄ mineral married at the molecular level with the metal. None of our spacecraft have windows, which you may have noticed. Not even our tough exoskeletons can take the pounding the stars extol for very long. No, I'm afraid your mighty little vessel's protections were about a thousand times too weak. I'm sorry to say, you wouldn't have lasted much past where we intercepted you. In fact, when I tricked the Constable into allowing me to perform my facsimile scan, you were nearly to the edge of your sun's heliosheath. If you had passed the heliopause and actually made it through the bowshock in your little tin can, and truly entered interstellar space, your bodies would have been eaten alive by cancer within a months' time. You never would have come close to reaching the sphere of icy little objects your star has collected on its trip around the galaxy. What do you refer to it as again? The Oort Cloud? It's not a cloud. It's more like a botchy sphere of—"

♓7ylÎx seemed to do the equivalent of clearing her throat.

☙9ylÎx nodded. "You're right, my <3. My apologies, Commander, Ms. Perle. I digress onto tangents quite easily and often."

"We never would have made it..." Don whispered.

☙9ylÎx shook her head. "You see? It's just one more reason the military should have simply left you be! This may sound cold, and I apologize in advance, but the problem would have taken care of itself. Your world would have learned of the crew's illness over the coming years as you relayed your status regularly, and your people would have realized they weren't ready to tackle interstellar space. There would be no more ships trying to leave the solar system. Not for a very long time, anyway."

Next to her, gurgling. Howling.

"Oh, I agree, ♓7y! I'm done with those amoeba-minded cockroaches. If the Constable had his way, there would be a spherical wall of plasma turrets all the way around the Sol system! All they had to do was fix the human ship, spin it around, give them a boost, reiterate the warning, and let them be on their way. But him, he's driven by ego and pride, and sees the world in black and white. He has zero room for *gray*."

The last howl sounded like a frog had given up and died.

"The Border Patrol!" ♋9ylÎx muttered. "To quote a famous French General of your history, 'They are an obstinate lot.'"

"France..." Adrienne said, staring off into space again. "I never made it to France." She looked up. "Ma'am—I'm sorry but I still can't pronounce your name—have you ever been to Earth?"

♋9ylÎx made a sound Don interpreted as a sigh. "I hate to admit it, but I've never set foot upon its surface. I've only enjoyed it from orbit. ♓7y, on the other hand, was a part of seven reconnaissance missions to your planet before the treaty came into being and policies were enacted. Before any physical contact with your species was forbidden.

She has regaled many stories of your vast rain forests and all the delicious plants and insects there!"

Exuberant chirping followed.

"Oh rub it in, why don't you!" she chided.

♓7ylÎx then emitted a series of chirps and clicks.

After she was finished, ♋9ylÎx turned all eyes to Don and Pearls. "She wants me to ensure you understand that she is not being rude by not speaking directly to you. She hasn't yet had her vocal chords modified in order to do so. Few have. It's a painful process."

More clicks and a screeching buzz reached Don's ears. He thought it somewhat painful in itself.

"Really?" exclaimed ♋9ylÎx. "That's wonderful!"

"What's wonderful?" asked Adrienne.

"♓7y just informed me that she has now decided to have the surgery, now that we will have humans to speak with in person on a regular basis! My <3, I'm so proud of you!"

The whirling and chirping that followed seemed exuberant. ♓7ylÎx top two appendages fluttered in the air.

"Wow," said Bouchard. "That seems like a tremendous sacrifice. I don't know what to say."

"Oh, just say 'It's about time!'" ♋9ylÎx rubbed a claw-like hand on ♓7ylÎx shell. "I've been hoping for this day for a ♍i1▷♑coy!"

"So," said Adrienne, "all the um, people in your society can understand us when we speak, they just can't physically make the sounds? I guess the Constable was struggling to even manage 'Go' and 'Earth' when he first spoke to us?"

"The Constable!" spat ♋9ylÎx. "We're fortunate he can say two words in our *own* tongue!"

Don laughed. "♋9ylÎx, you might tell your companion—or wife?—that my father's generation really had to fight to prevent those rainforests she spoke so fondly of from going the way of the dinosaurs. They're protected by international law now, so they'll still be there if she ever gets the chance to return to Earth."

"Well, well, look who's more observant than I gave him credit for!" ♋9ylÎx's mandibles spread wide, as if in a smile. "But ♓7ylÎx is not my wife as you define the word. Yes, we're companions, and we share living accommodations and the workload in our mini hive, but there is not a strict bond like the one you share with Ms. Treadwell. For instance, while we are very often by each other's side through 'thick and thin', I think is the term, we share a similar bond with several others in the lÎx hive. However, we do not marry nor mate like Earth companions do. Mating in our culture is a special ritual between select males and our Exalted Hive Queen, performed at regular intervals and on a tight schedule. ♓7ylÎx and myself are workers. Neither of us can bear offspring like the Queen can. But we don't die as early as the males do!"

"Similar to bees and ants," Pearls said. "In a way."

"Yes," said ♋9ylÎx. "Actually we're not that different from—"

Glurping and clicking emanated from ♓7ylÎx.

"Did I do it again? Oh. My apologies! Where was I?"

♓7ylîx chirped several times in rapid succession.

"Yes, thank you, I should mention that. Just so you two know, my next scheduled fake transmission will commence tomorrow morning."

"Your next what?" asked Adrienne.

"Commander, Ms. Perle, your people will become worried if you don't report in on a regular basis, correct?"

"I'd say that's a given," Don replied.

"And they may come looking for you?"

"Eventually."

"How often do you send updates?"

"Reports are expected at least daily. And we often send and respond to messages from friends and family as well."

"I assumed so," said ♓9ylîx. "Over the last seventy-seven of your hours, I've been faking your reports back to NASA and Space X headquarters, Commander. I first assured them everything is under control, that the 'non-natural source' you reported earlier was merely unusual radar reflections from a meteor storm, one that did zero damage to the ship. I told them this so they do not become alarmed and draw any unnecessary attention of the Border Patrol and the Council. NASA responded appropriately and no questions were asked that I could not answer. However, I feel I can only send so many of these messages before the Earthlings will become suspicious. I do not talk like you do, and I don't know personal things only you know. I thought I would ask, now that you're fully functional, would you like to start sending the reports yourself?"

"Surely you jest," said Pearls.

"Not at all."

She scoffed. "Okay. I assume you're sending text messages from the *Explorer Two's* computer?"

"No," ൭9ylÎx replied. "They are being transmitted from a moving beacon back to Earth that has exactly matched your spacecraft's last known speed and location."

"A beacon?" she repeated. "Why not use the ship itself? You could get the frequency wrong. The sine wave and the amplification. And NASA knows exactly where we are. If all these things aren't exactly like they've calculated, someone will take notice. They'll start asking questions. I thought you didn't want that before the big decision is made?"

Bouchard turned to Adrienne and studied her. "I'm impressed. I didn't know you paid that much attention to Ray's duties."

"It's a hobby," Pearls said. "I spend a lot of time with Ray. He has more patience than anyone I've ever met, and since he never sleeps or has any hobbies of his own, he's always at his station. Plus he can do a hundred things at once, so he can still do his work even when he's educating us "inferior beings", as he likes to jokingly put it. Sometimes I think he's serious."

Don smiled. "I can see that."

"All these things you mentioned have been taken care of, Ms. Perle," ൭9ylÎx assured her, ignoring their banter. "♓7y programmed the drone herself."

"But why?" asked Don. "Why the elaborate deception all of a sudden? Why not just use *Explorer Two's* systems?"

"For one thing, I do not have enough room in the hangar of the)I(J&)I(to recreate and assemble the *Explorer Two* piece-by-piece in my machine lab. For another, I am allowing you, and all your crew, to remain guests on my science vessel, which can take you wherever you want to go in a fraction of the time *Explorer Two* could have. Why would you want to travel throughout the galaxy inside such a slow machine?"

"Because it's our home," Adrienne said. "We don't need a recreation. We just want to go back to the actual spacecraft. We belong there. All our belongings and experiments are there."

"I can recreate some of the smaller items for you, if you wish," said ৯9ylÎx. "Even the experiments. The facsimile scan fully captured everything on board."

Adrienne's face scrunched up. "I don't get it. Why do you keep bringing up this recreation business? And that's three times now you mentioned a 'facsimile scan'. What is that?"

"I told that dung-headed roach it was standard procedure for the archives, if you remember. That was a lie, but he's too hard-shelled to actually read up on the protocols of my ministerial department. Oh don't worry even a bit, Ms. Perle. I not only gave you your natural legs back and removed all hint of those artificial cybernetics, I also repaired the recently-damaged DNA from your digital pattern! Our printer formed perfect strands in each and every one of your cells. Yours, too, Commander!"

Clicking noises came from ♓7ylÎx.

"Yes," said ♋9ylÎx, turning one eye to her wife, "a printer. I'm pretty sure that's what they call it." She then addressed Bouchard again. "That's correct, isn't it? You had similar although quite rudimentary devices on board your own vessel."

Bouchard stared at ♋9ylÎx.

"Please, there is nothing to be concerned about. You and every member of your crew will be fine, I promise you. In fact, not only are your bodies free of cancer, I corrected your chromosomes to their pre-treaty configuration! Isn't that wonderful? All of you could potentially live a thousand Earth years! Barring any accidents or disease or war, of course."

Clicking.

"Yes, ♓7y, or being discovered by the Border Patrol or the Royal Guard, which is basically what you would call the 'police' of this sector. Who would likely call for your immediate execution for being outside your quarantine zone in violation of the Earth-⊘♈*⌘↑m Pact. But we'll do our best to stay far away from them."

♓7ylÎx glurped and adjusted a glistening metal tendril. A series of purple dots appeared overhead, overlaid on what appeared to be a star map.

♋9ylÎx pointed overhead. "These purple globes represent the Royal Guard. We will plot a path around them. And speaking of disease," she continued, "when your doctor wakes up, you can ensure her that she doesn't have to worry about any of us contracting something from the other. I've used ♓7y's data from her visits to Earth to not only protect us from your pathogens, but also you from ours!"

♓7ylîx almost squawked.

"Well of course I'm proud of myself!" ♋9ylîx replied, waving several wiry appendages about. "I'd like to see my egotistical sister do any of that! She and all the other 9y series might be good at stellar navigation, but none of them can weave deoxyribonucleic acid like I can!"

Bouchard wanted to ask something, but his jaw merely opened and closed, and nothing came out. He was almost afraid to ask any more questions, afraid of the answers. For instance, he could read a few of the symbols in the star map. Locations of enemy vessels. Identifications of stars.

"Of course the one you call X-Ray would be much more interested in all of this talk! For him I naturally had to make zero adjustments! His synthetic body would not have been significantly affected by the interstellar radiation, at least not in this sector. He could hypothetically have made it all the way to the Centauri system, had your tiny tin can actually held up for the next five or ten thousand of your years, and had the military allowed it. For a moment I thought they were actually going to let him and the ship continue on, considering he is not exactly 'human'. But, the Constable reasoned, he was designed, built, and programmed by humans, so he was just as likely as serious a threat as you all were."

Bouchard blinked. It was all he could manage.

"No matter. With machines, as I mentioned before, our ability to create an exact copy is one hundred percent. With organic matter, however, especially advanced life forms such as yourselves, I'm sad to report that errors do enter the system. So unfortunate; the facsimiles are never one hundred percent like the original. 91.5 percent on average, but never a hundred." The alien shook her head.

Don swallowed. *What is she saying?*

♓7ylÎx rested a claw on ♌9ylÎx's thorax, and chirped quietly.

♌9ylÎx's head tiled sideways. "Of course, my dear, of course. Please ignore me, Commander, Ms. Perle. I should not be discussing such things in front of you, and I won't do so in front of your crew."

Bouchard was numb. He looked at his hands. Turned them over once. They looked the same as they always did. He put a hand to his chest. Felt his heart thumping there. The taste in his mouth, the one he couldn't quite make out. Being able to make out some symbols of the aliens' language without being taught. Things were starting to explain themselves.

"My legs?" Don turned to see Pearls squeezing her hips, then her thighs, her knees, her shins. Her breathing quickened, and a tear rolled down her cheek. "Not my magical legs..."

Bouchard could only stare at her as she repeated the process, seemingly trying to verify that all her prized cybernetics were indeed gone. Sure, he himself had lived with the heart of an android, his wife had her crystal blue, cybernetic eyes, and the others had various small artificialities. But no one had fully-actuated prosthetic limbs like Adrienne. They set her apart from the pack. They made her a superhero. Now, she was as normal as everyone else. His heart, his now human heart, ached in sympathy as he watched her crumple to the floor in tears.

"By the way, Ray Isley's facsimile is being constructed in a different lab than yours, our machine lab. It's just down the hall. I will allow you inside now. I will allow you inside each of the labs. You can go in and see your android being reconstructed!"

Don's blank stare shifted to the alien woman.

"I think you'd find the process extremely fascinating," ♋9ylÎx went on, "even though you aren't the science officer."

"Donnie," Adrienne whispered between sobs, "if she's saying what I think she's saying... where are our *souls!?*"

One of ♋9ylÎx's many appendages touched a mandible. "In hindsight, I should have re-constructed Mr. Isley first, so he could observe the others being 'birthed'. Oh, he would have enjoyed it so!" She turned to her companion. "Now why didn't you think of that?"

♓7ylÎx shook her head, clicked twice, and pointed at the display boasting the colored circles that ♋9ylÎx had checked earlier.

"What?" ♋9ylÎx asked, leaning over the console to see. "Oh yes, thank you! Look at that timing. Right about now, Commander, the next two members of your crew should be nearing completion. Would you like to greet them as they wake up? One is your lovely wife."

ELEVEN

OFFICIAL ⦸♈*⌘↑m INCIDENT REPORT:
Rendezvous with *Explorer Two*
DATE: ♍i1^ 3.2, ▷♑coy 625-N23 (7 May, 2177, Earth Common Era)

Vessel: Name: *Explorer Two.* Type: Exploration, non-military. Design and construction: Earth, civilian/government project (multi-national). Perpetrators involved: United States, United Kingdom, China, Japan, Canada, France, Germany, Australia, Russia, India.

Crew: Seven. Three married couples, one synthetic human. In order of command structure:

Donald *"Donnie Darko"* Bouchard. Male. Mission Commander, Canadian.

Adrienne *"Pearls"* Perle-Liev. Female. Pilot/First Officer, Indian.

Jack *"Scales"* Scalia. Male. Navigator, American.

Lawrence *"Mag-Lev"* Liev. Male. Mission Specialist, Russian-American.

Brea *"Treads"* Treadwell-Bouchard. Female. Payload Specialist, British.

Melodi *"M&M"* Meng-Scalia. Female. Medical Specialist, Chinese-American.

Ray *"X-Ray"* Isley. Android. Science Specialist, No Nationality.

Primary mission: Exploration of the interstellar medium immediately past ♏42☼3⃠♈=⊗'s Heliopause.

Secondary mission: Locate and revive Voyager 2 spacecraft, catch and release. Launched ♍i1^2.4, ▷♑coy 625-N23 (20 August 1977, Earth Common Era).

Tertiary mission: Continue on toward Alpha Centauri system, past natural lives of human crew; synthetic humanoid crewmember was prepared to transmit data to Earth as long as *Explorer Two* remained viable.

Armament: Deuterium-based fusion missiles (six), each with multiple warheads (ten). Yield: 0.42153 ♎☼ (Earth measurement: 310 megatons per missile). Analysis: Ineffective against most Royal Military vessels with Class 2 or higher rating. May cause minor damage to civilian liners. Likely intended use: self-defense against natural threats.

Armor: None. Of note: Superstructure of *Explorer Two* neared failure upon seizure by Border Patrol using speed-retardant particle beam. At lowest setting.

Current or last-known location: Grid (x)=58362952, Base (y)=32*C1, Elevox (z)=T51☼3655. Heliosheath (edge of Earth's solar system).

Current status of vessel: Destroyed by Border Patrol. Reason: departure of quarantined territory of ♏42☼3⦸♈=⊗ System, thus breaking the Earth-⦸♈*⌘↑m Pact of Human King Solomon Era (6542 K.S.E.), prior to Earth's last Ice Age.

Current status of crew: Deceased.

END OF OFFICAL REPORT
SUBMITTED BY
৯9ylîx, HIVE Iîx
PRIMARY ⦸♈*)(*♈⦸ ATTACHÉ TO EARTH

Glossary of Select Terms

♋9ylÎx
Overseer attaché to Earth, pronounced "Senine-y-lix"

♓7ylÎx
Companion of ♋9ylÎx, pronounced "Beeseven-y-lix"

lÎx
Hive of ♋9y and ♓7y

)I(J&)I(
♋9y and ♓7y's science and research vessel, named "J&"

☪3uiÎp
The former attaché to Earth, pronounced "Kaythree-uee-ip"

▷♑coy
211.1 Earth years

♍i1▷♑coy
53.7 Earth years

♑♏
The equivalent of 34.7 Earth days

⦸♈*)(*♈⦸
The Overseer Council of Federated Worlds in the galaxy

⦸♈*⌘↑m
The Overseer Treaty, initiated by Hive ⌘↑m

nano♌♒
Overseer nanotechnology

♎☼

A quantity of explosive yield measurement

♑x(*)

A quantum electromagnetic device that draws energy from the vacuum of space

☼⌅❄

A protective mineral embedded in Overseer spacecraft hulls

♏42☼3⦸♈=⊗

Earth (with "Forbidden X" indicator)

♍i1

A small fraction of time, perhaps a minute

⭯eT↕

(You don't want to know)

♐B&

A replication matrix used by the Overseer Empire

mUu❖i

A silly little thing, given to insectoid offspring as a toy, but deemed intensely fascinating and valuable to humans

Grid, Base, Elevox

A three-dimensional grid coordinate system

Dear reader,

May I ask a favor? I would be thrilled if you could hop over to Amazon.com and post a super quick review of Border Patrol. Good or bad, either is fine; like I've often said, an honest review is even better than a pound of warm, delicious bacon. But just barely.

Also, I entertain all cool sci fi and speculative fiction ideas. e-mail me! rod@rodwerks.net

And remember, please visit RodWerks.net/SecretSC to read or obtain a free download of the first fifteen pages of my military sci-fi novel, **Distress Call**! ☺

Rod Galindo
August, 2017

Thank you for reading Border Patrol.

I hope you enjoyed it!

Now, please enjoy this excerpt from my military science fiction novelette, ***The Tesla Project: 1975***

I

Sergeant First Class Mike Tyler touched his earpiece to activate the embedded microphone. "Raven Rock Command, this is Traveler Three, commo check, over."

"Roger, Traveler Three, read you Lima Charlie," came the tinny reply from a random technician, indicating the command center could hear him "loud and clear."

He adjusted the weight on his back, a modified U.S. Army-issue rucksack. It was half empty to allow room for to-be-acquired items but was still heavy, mainly thanks to the working guts of a mini rocketpack the U.S. Army of 2025 allowed him to bring back with him. Not to mention its fuel.

"All departments report GO," announced a civilian wearing a colorful shirt and even louder tie, sitting just over a hundred meters in front of Tyler in a theater-style room. The man and a dozen other military and civilian personnel sat or stood, viewing him through a narrow, rectangular window. "Traveler Three, Standby."

Director Johansen's voice boomed in his ear. "Traveler Three, you are authorized to load your weapons."

"Roger, RAVROCOM." He first loaded a thirty-round magazine into the standard Army-issue M-16 that his superiors all but forced him to take along, and "charged" the rifle to load a round into the chamber. He left the weapon on "Safe" because he didn't trust it; one violent bump and the damn thing had a habit of discharging on its own. He was about to take it through a rift in spacetime; he didn't want to imagine what throwing a piece of lead off into the quantum foam—he'd heard it called that once—might do to the universe. There were more trustworthy future upgrades of the rifle, such as the M-16A1, the M-16A2, and even the M-4 and its various incarnations; his fellow travelers had brought them back for study and he had seen American soldiers carrying them on his many trips to the future. But would General West allow him to use those? *Of course he won't.*

After much back and forth, he was finally allowed to keep his favorite pistol, a .50 caliber Desert Eagle he'd obtained from a trip to 2005. "Betty", as he called the satin-black Mark XIX, combined the power of a revolver with the characteristics of a rifle all soldiers were familiar with, the aforementioned standard Army-issue M-16. These attributes made it the most powerful semi-automatic pistol the world had seen, even up through 2025. He slapped a seven-round magazine into Betty and charged her to send a round into the chamber, but intentionally left the safety off; Tyler had no fear of Betty coughing up a round when he didn't want her to do so. He then re-holstered the ten-inch, polygonal-barreled hand cannon, built to bore through car engine blocks, and touched his earpiece again. "Ready."

"Roger, Traveler Three," replied the Director.

"Coordinates set," he heard someone announce. "Capacitors at ninety-nine percent. Supercoolers are GREEN. Initializing temporal core."

Tyler experienced a slight disorientation as the round platform he stood upon freed itself from the only physical object holding it in place—a long, thick chrome pillar, which was currently out of his sight. In his mind's eye he could see the pillar dropping into the lowest point of the sphere, one hundred meters beneath him. He steadied himself; now only powerful rare-Earth magnets in the platform kept it, and him, from plummeting over three hundred feet to the sea of lightning rods jutting up from below like stalagmites from a cavern floor. Hundreds of similar rods jutted from every direction he looked. A one-hundred-meter walkway to his right, leading to the platform upon which he stood, began its painfully slow retraction.

"Core at twenty percent," said the civilian in the technicolor shirt. "Thirty. Fifty. Supercoolers dipping slightly, still well within nominal levels."

The walkway clicked when it completed its journey into the wall just beneath the only door out of the huge spherical room.

"Initiating Relocation Gyros," said another tech.

Sergeant Tyler's heart pumped harder as three large, circular rings lifted from their resting place around the central platform, not unlike the rings around Saturn. They began to rotate around themselves, around *him*. The largest ring was so big, it spun only a few meters from the inner wall. The middle ring spun inside the large ring. The third and smallest ring was close, too close for Tyler's comfort. The result of this array was three rings spinning independently of each other, all on different vectors, in a dizzying dance. Tyler focused on the control room; he learned long ago not to look too long at those damned rings, they would just make him queasy.

A wind picked up, generated by the motion of the rings. Tyler's gaze rose to the lightning rods above him in anticipation. *There they are!* The blue-violet stars. He couldn't help but smile at the sight, as the tip of each rod all around the Temporal Sphere glowed with Saint Elmo's Fire in the dense magnetic field generated by the spinning blades. The "fire" created a buzzing that grew in intensity with the wind and made the breeze smell tinny from ionization.

"Translocation Gyros stable, speed at target parameters, Einstein-Rosen horizon rising," said the colorful civilian. "Transferring coordinates to TRM computer."

TRM. Time Relocation Mechanism. Mike Tyler often chuckled that something with such a name was actually a part of his duty description. Who would have ever guessed?

He had never been in a tornado, but he guessed this was what one felt like. A tiny one, at least. He pulled the bill of his helmet, or "Kevlar", down over his eyes and crouched to make himself a smaller target, less aerodynamic so as not to be swept off the platform.

A new voice filtered into his ear now. "Now's not the time to be sucking your thumb, Mike."

Tyler cocked his head slightly and eye-balled the far right end of the giant rectangular window before him. There stood his commander and friend, Major Matthew Wilson, observing the trip. "Asshole," he muttered without keying his mic.

He saw Wilson lean over and speak into one of the microphones. "Say again, Traveler Three, we didn't quite catch that." As usual Wilson wore his Army Class A dress uniform instead of the slightly dressed-down Class B which most other military personnel wore at the facility. His jacket and pants were impeccable, creased in all the right places. A stack of service and campaign ribbons, most of which he had been awarded for various tours to Vietnam, nearly reached his collarbone.

Tyler touched his earpiece this time to activate the microphone. "Just said I'm ready to go," he shouted, so as to be heard over the wind and the buzzing of the glowing rods.

Wilson laughed, silently from Tyler's perspective.

Director Johansen spoke into his ear now. "Sergeant Tyler, initiate hover mode. One-half thrust."

This marked a change in standard procedure. On every occasion before now, Tyler simply jumped through an open rift above the round platform like he was walking through a doorway. This time he was forced to do things a little differently. He opened a small green box on his heavy, olive-drab-green utility belt and removed what looked like the grip of a gun, minus the barrel. With his thumb he pressed the red glowing button on top of the hand grip and heard the click and whir of two gimbaling rocket nozzles extending from either side of his rucksack. He squeezed the trigger. The tiny rockets ignited, filling the sphere with light and exhaust. He mashed the trigger with more force, and his feet lifted from the ground. He listed sideways almost immediately. *Oh boy. Wilson was right, I should have practiced more.* He struggled to hover in one place over the windy platform.

"Steady, Mike!" he heard Wilson shout in his ear.

"I got it," he shouted back, fighting the handgrip, flying back and forth and forth and back, doing everything he could to keep himself mostly above the platform. At one point he turned his head just in the nick of time to prevent decapitation from one of the spinning rings and a very bad day for all involved.

"Open the rift now!" Wilson ordered.

"Not yet, sir," replied Johansen, "the core is only at..." he checked a readout. "Ninety-two percent. We need to be at least to ninety eight so the—"

"Open it before he's blown into those damned rings!"

Tyler heard nothing more, but could easily imagine the scowl on the Director's face. A second later, the inside edge of each spinning ring exploded with blinding white light. Before him grew the familiar swirl of a rip in spacetime. Blue smoky filaments extended from somewhere unseen around him and were then sucked into nowhere.

"Godspeed, my friend!" Wilson said in his ear. "If my older self greets you *this* time, tell that geezer it's time to retire, for Chrissakes!"

Tyler gave his commander a nod he wasn't sure was caught. He steered himself into the vortex before him. As usual, the world turned white, the most brilliant white he had ever experienced. It reminded Mike of the "Teller Light" that he read about, which occurred in the microseconds just after a nuclear explosion. A light brighter than the sun. He had once heard a rumor he couldn't quite believe, but which fascinated him nevertheless. It concerned what one of the scientists present at the Bikini Atoll detonation in 1954 said, the one without goggles who had his back to the mushroom cloud and was watching the other scientists. This man—Tyler couldn't remember his name—claimed that at the moment the "Castle Bravo" bomb went off, the flash of light was so bright that he could see the skull and jawbone of each man, as if seeing their heads in an x-ray image. The light was called the "Teller Light", after Edward Teller who had helped engineer the

U.S.A.'s first fifteen megaton "super" thermonuclear device.

But there was a much more groovy effect than ridiculously bright light during each 'jump'. Each time Tyler entered the cloud, the white world was there, but it always lingered much longer than it should. It was like watching a film in slow-motion, only he was in the film. He surmised that time itself slowed down as he traveled through the rift, but the scientists assigned to the Tesla Project didn't believe him. He had no proof; all the time-keeping instruments he took with him—including his watch—never strayed even a millisecond from those back in the project control room. For everyone else, his trip was instantaneous. For him, it lasted a good five seconds. He suspected this happened to the other travelers as well, but if so, they never admitted to it. In fact, they laughed at him when he brought it up. They called it "Tyler's Disney Land." Their teasing made Mike wonder if he was indeed crazy. Perhaps it didn't really happen, perhaps it *was* all just in his head.

Regardless if his Disney Land was real or not, he still wondered about the Teller Light. If someone were to ever go into the rift with him, would that person see Tyler's bones? And if so, would history call it the "Tyler Light", after the first guy to ever wonder about it?

A young enlisted man could dream.

Tyler was through. The crackling of the lightning remained, but the wind was gone. Before him was nothing but blackness. Tyler's head jerked from left to right, but nothing met his eyes save for tiny blue stars all around him, and occasionally a bolt of lightning danced from one point to another point behind him, presumably into the wormhole. Or was it the other way around?

The darkness was expected, but was still jarring and unusual, especially with his feet no longer planted on solid ground. He focused on the tiny blue stars, but had a hard way of telling if he was falling or zooming toward that inner wall ahead of him. He did his best to center the hand grip to ensure he had no trajectory of any kind, but it didn't help his nerves. He rotated the rocketpack's handgrip to the right, which rotated him 180 degrees. Now facing the opposite way, he found the red-tinted vortex exactly where it was supposed to be, which replaced the blue one from a moment ago. "There you are."

With it, he at least had solid bearings again, and a confirmation he was indeed motionless, hovering in mid-air. He tried to look past the dimly glowing red portal to 1975, which would remain open until closed by his friends back in that era. It swirled like cigarette smoke in a room with a draft. But other than it, he couldn't see much. The Temporal Sphere looked just like it had a few seconds ago, minus the spinning rings. The lightning rods here in this time all had the same blue-violet glow; the little stars that quieted his soul.

He caught something out of the corner of his eye. A patch of the sphere was illuminated below him. He looked downward, but could see little past his body armor. He nudged the flight control stick forward, then made a slow bank to the left, flying around the vortex. This allowed him to turn his head to the left and look down. The rings were all there, stowed in place and motionless, as they should be, held in place by two giant mounts jutting from opposite walls. The inner ring was in his way, so he flew a little farther out, where he could see through the large gap between it and the middle ring. *There!* A single beam of light illuminated the lowest point of the sphere.

The camera.

The spotlight mounted to the large low-tech video camera the U.S. Army had sent into the Einstein-Rosen Bridge, or E-R Bridge, the day prior lay on the floor one hundred meters below him. Tyler reminded himself it had actually arrived here only seconds ago, relatively speaking, regardless of when it had been sent. The camera itself was in pieces, destroyed by the fall. No matter, it had done its job as pathfinder, saving *him* from being destroyed by the same fall. In the three seconds it had transmitted its video—yesterday by his frame of reference, only moments ago by its own—it had verified that any traveler would indeed need something to prevent a nasty fall if he or she were to survive more than three seconds on this trip. Hence the authorization to use the rocketpack this time.

Something crossed his mind. *The walkway.* He looked over his shoulder to find it retracted. *Odd.* This was not standard operating procedure; when the blades had no reason to spin, as in the case of a receiving sphere, the walkway was always extended to the platform in the receiving time period. The platform was also always there to prevent a traveler from falling to his or her death. Looking more closely, he could make out the platform's outline on the floor; the camera had bounced off it when it made its crash landing.

Crash. This sparked alarm in Tyler's head. The Temporal Sphere was heavily insulated against sound, so the tearing noise generated by ripping the fabric of space and time, the crashing sound of the large camera, plus the roar of his rocketpack *could* have announced his arrival to anyone who might be in the immediate area outside the sphere, but not elsewhere in the facility. But thanks to the large rectangular window—which was actually six inches of clear metal rather than actual glass—the sphere did *not* insulate against visible light. And his rocketpack was generating a lot of light right now. His head snapped toward the control room. Enough light shone in there that he could easily make out familiar chairs and consoles. So could anyone else either in there or in the hallway off the control room, especially if the door to the hall was open and they happened to be anywhere near the sphere. It was time to head for the exit and minimize his "noise and light pollution."

Using slight movements of the grip, he steered himself toward the door. A wire-mesh catwalk ran around the equator of the room, just as it had in 1975, and was wide enough for two people to stand next to each other comfortably. Releasing the trigger, his right foot touched down on the catwalk, then his left. He pressed the red button on the handgrip again, and the small rockets cut off and snapped back into his ruck. Tyler assumed a crouched fighting stance and raised his rifle. He ceased all movements and listened. Nothing stirred except the gentle "breathing" of the still-open E-R Bridge, and the occasional crackle of electricity. Now only blackness filled the glass of the control room. A clap of thunder created by a rather nasty static discharge snapped him from his trance.

Tyler keyed his mic. "Raven Rock Command, this is Traveler Three, over."

"The...he is!" he heard someone say. It sounded like Director Johansen.

Major Wilson broke in. "Tra...ler Three, this is RAVR...OM, we read y..." The transmission was broken, but readable. "Gla... you made......ere safe. SITREP."

Tyler understood Wilson wanted a report on his situation. "Roger, RAVROCOM. I made it here in better shape than the camera did, that's for sure," Tyler said. "SITREP follows: Currently in the Temporal Sphere. Both the sphere and Control Room are dark and dusty, no power. The air is stale but breathable. No sign of hostiles. Or friendlies for that matter. Preparing to cut through the door to the sphere and explore the facility and surrounding area. How copy?"

"Rog.......Traveler Three. Copy: sphere is...thout power, environme...al condition GREEN, prepp...ing to explore facil... Be advised, portal...re-open...cisely at 1500."

Tyler checked his digital watch. It read "11:03 18 MAY 75." He had just under four hours to find out what he could about this era and get back to the sphere to return home. Lieutenant Stark gave him very detailed instructions in the mission brief yesterday. *More like pounded them into my head.* His thumb engaged the mic. "Roger."

"No sign of......older self anywhe...?" asked Wilson, breaking standard radio protocol.

"Negative," Tyler replied.

"I'll take that as...ood sign; mayb......old bugger...inally retired!"

"Or he's kicked it."

Wilson ignored that. "Goo...luck, Mike, see you in four ho......AVROCOM out."

A second later, Tyler heard a deep *puff*. He glanced over his shoulder to see the glowing red smoke dissipate into the darkness at the center of the sphere and one by one, the tiny bluish flames on each lightning rod winked out. He was now immersed in total darkness, and was very much on his own.

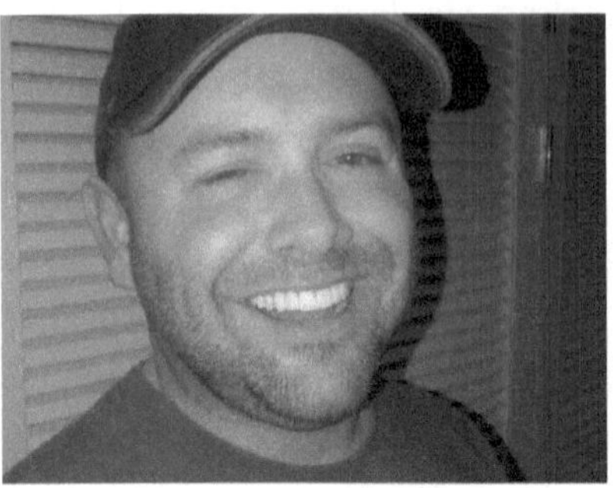

About the Author

Rod A. Galindo arrived on Earth in the Spring of 1970. He's been trying to stay out of trouble ever since, but has now accepted it as one of the three things he does well, right behind drawing and right ahead of spelling. He's beamed all around the world thanks to various military and government positions, but proudly calls Kansas City home. Mainly because his request for transfer to Stargate Command was denied. AGAIN.

"Major Galindo" has nearly thirty years of service under his belt in the U. S. Army, both Active Duty (as an enlisted M-1A1 Abrams tank crewman, Operation Desert Storm) and the Kansas Army National Guard (as a Field Artillery officer, Operation Noble Eagle, Operation Iraqi Freedom, and now Operation Inherent Resolve).

"Rod Galindo" is a worn-out father of four; two cyber-smart teenaged boys, one German Army (Bundeswehr) Soldatin who is as dangerously clever as she is beautiful, and he fills in as full-time father to a special young lady who never really had a dad to call her own.

Rod is a fully assimilated and very active member of the Wordwraiths Writing Collective and Wordwraith Books, LLC (learn more about our authors and books at Wordwraiths.com). Enjoy his shiny art or delve into his literary musings at RodWerks.net or RodGalindo.com.

www.ingramcontent.com/pod-product-compliance
Lightning Source LLC
Chambersburg PA
CBHW051953170626
46808CB00007B/2594
9781946921031